About the Author

I'm a seventy-year-old African-American man, with a diverse background of multiple careers and hobbies; from accounting, sales and insurance, to business owner, golfer and aviator. Married with six children and four grandchildren. During the Covid-19 shut down, I felt compelled to write down my longstanding story ideas, which had vexed me for many years. The result of my musing is 'Mission 53'.

Mission 53

Lester Bynum

Mission 53

Olympia Publishers
London

www.olympiapublishers.com
OLYMPIA PAPERBACK EDITION

A CIP catalogue record for this title is
available from the British Library.

ISBN: 978-1-80439-497-7

This is a work of fiction.
Names, characters, places and incidents originate from the writer's
imagination. Any resemblance to actual persons, living or dead, is
purely coincidental.

First Published in 2023

Olympia Publishers
Tallis House
2 Tallis Street
London
EC4Y 0AB

Printed in Great Britain

Dedication

I dedicate this book to my lovely and inspirational wife Heather Bynum. To my children and grandchildren, I hope you enjoy this story and think of me fondly when you read it.

Lester Calvin Bynum

Acknowledgements

Much thanks must go to my wife for her encouragement and editorial support and for her patience in allowing much of what remained in this book, to stay in this book. And to Eder Santos for his exceptional illustrations, which may not be included in this initial book distribution.

PREFACE

In the beginning of space and time, planet GREY3110227 came into existence at the Big Bang.

The beings which live upon planet GREY (capital letters) are called greys[12] (lower case letters).

They have evolved successfully after discovering and preserving an inscribed plaque. The discovered plaque's inscription reads as follows:

"Sector: **GREY** Destination: **3110227** Galaxy: ✿∞ᐯ⊢⟨ "

Along with the following inscribed definition:

"At the **BIG BANG**, all matter was cast asunder, into **INFINITY**. This world is known to reside at the **SOUTH GREY Sector**. Specifically, into **Destination: 3110227**. The ultimate inhabitants will become, **TRAVELERS[28]**." ~~ **ABOVE** ~~

Evolutionary instructions taught throughout many generations, by other peaceful Travelers,[28] spanning the Solar Systems from other planets, is how the greys learned the life sustaining message of:

Peace, Love, and Harmony.

As they have evolved to become Travelers themselves, zoom missions to millions of other Planets, throughout these past millions of years they have been very successful in efforts to do as they've been instructed. Which is to communicate Peace, Love, and Harmony to any "Seeking"[24] inhabitants of any world.

Recent IPC[14] communications from other solar systems have confirmed that Planet Blue is not long for the Universe. If their creatures continue their most recent actions with nuclear explosions, and other harmful planetary acts, they may trigger the opening of their planet's core by way of fissures, which could rend their planets mantle. This would result in the planet becoming the latest and brightest starlite to ignite into oblivion from within their Galaxy.

Inhabitants of Planet Blue remain unresponsive to previous attempts at peaceful communications and are continuing along their observed pathways of distrust, fear, hatred, and destruction.

Today's Zoom Mission Convoy is in the final stages of preparation.

Upon Planet GREY3110227, Plates[23] are being prepared for the latest Zoom Mission Convoy[34] to Planet Blue.

Multiple plumes from explosions, volcanic eruptions, and smoke from worldly fires have infected the cosmos. These activities are clearly signs of planetary distress.

Today's Zoom Mission to the blue planet aims at their inhabitants, for furthering the attempts to communicate with its intelligent beings. We are seeking to impart our message to its inhabitants.

Keeping them from self-annihilation is part one of their two-part mission. Secondly, teaching them to become peaceful beings within the whole of the Universe, co-existing harmoniously with all other planets, is why these missions must continue.

Persuading, through voluntary acceptance, any level of intelligence found upon any planet is our mission. Therefore, all life forms which are willing to adopt the espoused principles of Peace, Love, and Harmony contribute to the cornerstone of harmonious galactic co-existence and our Zoom Mission goals.

This latest mission to Planet Blue, continues...

[Reference Glossary for terminology and superscript references]

Chapter 1

BLUE TODAY

Zak was walking down a corridor. In his left hand he was holding his Flight Guide Orb (FGO), reading today's flight plan while sipping sugar from the sugar cane stalk he grabbed on his way out of the commissary. He was headed to the Departure Prep Facility (DPF). He needed to flush his system, get sprayed, and be in his craft, ready for neuro-connectivity within the next twenty-five minutes. Today's Zoom Mission would give Zak his first opportunity to make firsthand observations of the images he and the rest of the world have previously only been able to view on a screen. This would be Zak's fifty-third Zoom Mission, but his first to Planet Blue.

Commander Kray greeted Zak as he entered the DPF building. "Get a move on rookie. We're not gonna wait for you!" he barked.

"Yes, Sir!" Zak replied. "I'm moving." Zak tossed his chewed cane stalk into the trash receptacle just inside the door and turns left to enter the body flushing zone. Once inside, attendants direct Zak to his stall and there were about thirty NSD's and TST's in the adjoining stalls with their attendants. The Directors and TST's were on tables as they were being connected to flush pumps and monitors. Zak tossed his FGO onto the counter and hopped up onto the table and was immediately transitioned into unconsciousness. He was awakened in seven minutes, sat up and waited for his head to clear before hopping down and moving on to the showers.

It was always funny to Zak looking at how his body appeared after the flushing procedure. Due to the extraction of so much liquid from his body, he felt like he was wearing a heavy, purple spotted fur coat.

"Don't forget to grab your FGO as you exit the showers, Sir," one of his attendants reminded him.

"Okay, will do. Thanks," Zak replied while thinking to himself, "I really appreciate the redundancies throughout this facility." He knew that on his way out of the building, anything he'd left behind in his flushing cube would be waiting for him as he exited, with yet another friendly reminder from an attendant.

As Zak walked toward the showers tram, he crisscrossed in-between some TST Directors as they were jockeying to get into their adjacent tram lines. Zak headed left, stepping onto his tram just behind a couple of other Directors. Looking to his right, he observed the TST's on their tram. The TST's basically received the same shower coating that chemically shrunk and dried their furry bodies, creating that smooth, slender, gray skin pre-flight shape as the NSD's. But, the TST's tram had an extra kink in it. The difference was an S Curve in the tram which took the TST's through an X-Ray scanner. It flashed once to confirm their translucence. After exiting the scanner tube, every TST would reflexively trigger a responding bright flash from within their own bodies as they exited the scanner. Their bodies were thoroughly sprayed, front, back, top, and bottom as they were transported along the tram. The tram showers and transport process took all of three minutes to complete.

On the way out of the DPF building an attendant reminded Zak, "Don't forget your FGO, Sir, and have a great flight."

As Zak grabbed his Orb, he thanked the attendant and said,

"Will do." Zak and all NSD Pilots exited left toward the fifty Plates that were in various stages of final flight preparations.

All the Plates were affixed to the departure ramp. Surprisingly, Zak noticed a couple of TST's (Sean Westix and Shay Kromblay) turning left to join his NSD squadron of Plate Directors. All other TST's turned right heading toward their high intensity non-luminous ORB crafts. About sixty ORB crafts were hovering about three feet above their ramp pads with no attendants refueling or handling any of them. This would be the first Zoom Mission Convoy for Zak that included TST's directing Plates rather than ORBs. Walking to his assigned Plate, Zak reflected on the progress of his previous fifty-two missions. Due to his former success, he felt proud to be one of the planet's premiere citizens. This was Zak's first mission to Blue. He was excited to be in the convoy and had absolutely no expectations. The overhead announcement and flashing lights signaled it was time for the final countdown phase of the mission preparations. Zak greeted his Plate attendant, "All systems go, Jay?"

"Yes, Sir, I'll finalize sealings once you're secure and neuro-connected," Jay responded.

"Great, thanks," Zak replied as he walked up the ramp and leaned back into his standing flight command chair.

"ATTENTION, ATTENTION!" Lights flashed as the announcement blared on the ramp speakers. "EIGHT MINUTES TO LIFT OFF, EIGHT MINUTES TO LIFT OFF!" Zak placed his FGO into its circular holder next to his right-hand control pad, (which is where he placed his hand to switch on the neuro-connectivity process). The Plate craft extended its tentacles from the ceiling and floor to engulf and effectively absorb Zak. They were now one, no longer Director and Plate craft, just Plate.

"ATTENTION, ATTENTION!" lights flashed again as the

16

announcement blared on the ramp speakers. "TWO MINUTES TO LIFT OFF, TWO MINUTES TO LIFT OFF!" Jay, having visually confirmed Zak's successful neuro-connectivity, completed the external chemical sealings of the Plate, and removed himself along with the other straggling attendants from the ramp departure area. Commander Kray confirmed all fifty Plates reflecting green GO indicators on his forward-looking monitor (or control panel). He intimated a thought communications check for all Directors. "Prepare for departure." Commander Kray's intimated communication hit the brains of each Director, with no words, just thought. The Directors instantaneous thought responses confirmed readiness for departure.

Fifty Planet GREY3110227 non-shape shifting Plates slowly began rising in unison from their departure deck stations. When all Plates, formed an absolute and precisely straight line between them, reached sixty feet above deck surface...

There was a solid blinding flash of brilliant light across all fifty Planetary crafts which made absolutely no sound. Gone. Not even a vapor trail was left. There was simply nothing there. The Zoom Mission Convoy had instantly transitioned from stationary hovering objects to enroute crafts, blazing toward Planet Blue.

Chapter 2

THE ARRIVAL

Having a creative mind that can imagine what it would be like to travel from place to place by thought alone, was enthralling. Experiencing the process of traveling by thought alone, is mind blowing. Understandably, NSD pilots found it exhilarating to experience Zoom speeds. Using Zoom speeds for the upcoming trip to the Blue Planet allowed the convoy to arrive within the hour, covering fifty-three million light years. Commander Kray had been imparting instructions and post departure communications to all convoy NSD's throughout the flight via neuro-connective thought transference. If there was vital information, or details for the Directors, Commander Kray would merely intimate a communication. Acknowledgements and responses were sent back in turn by thoughts or communicative intimations. It is a wonderous thing to be neurologically linked to an intelligent craft.

In a Plates convoy of any size, all crafts are synchronized to their Commanders thought waves. The connection eliminates communication errors. Plates are so agile and responsive to thought commands, collisions are virtually impossible. The illuminated line attached to the Blue Planet indicated the convoy was closing fast. Zak's 3D forward-looking monitor started to blink, and the Blue Planet became significantly larger within the space between his standing command chair and his display panel. Just as Zak was beginning to think Planetary collision could be a real possibility, he clearly understood/heard his commander's announcement...

"Attention! Attention! Prepare for Zoom disengagement!"

Immediately, as if brakes were being applied to slow his Plate, Zak's 3D display disappeared by retracting into his forward-looking monitor. His display screen clicked on, revealing the Blue Planet steadily growing, but now, at a slower speed. Zak's front, sides and rear panels phased to opaque. He observed that the whole convoy had stopped in mid-air. The convoy was eighty miles above the Blue Planet. They had arrived.

On the Commander's orders, all Plates moved to their assigned quadrants above the planet, maintaining eighty miles above its surface. Zak's Plate was repositioned by Commander Kray's thought, to a specific quadrant directly above the very bright Blue Planet. Zak observed the dispersal of the crafts, disseminated, and spread out completely around the planet.

He immediately felt lonely. He was hovering with all his visual panels set to opaque or opened for "Inside Out" viewing. Zak momentarily enjoyed the views. He looked all around, bathed in the soft blue light from the planet as it cast its reflection toward the dark blackness of open space. He couldn't see another Plate anywhere, except on the 3D imagery from his forward-looking monitor.

"Prepare for descent," Commander Kray intimated. Without warning, Zak's Plate Zoomed from hovering eighty miles above the Planet's surface, to a three thousand-feet above ground hover. His Plate materialized above a sector that looked like a city. "NSD control now authorized. Good luck!" Commander Kray said telepathically.

"Thank you, Sir," Zak thought in response to his

commander. Zak reached up with his right hand and flicked his Plate Command toggle switch to ON. Now he had one hundred percent control of his Plate through his own thought commands.

"Welcome, Director ZAK!" his Plate intimated to him.

"Hi. Thanks!" Zak thought back, as he was unbuckling himself from his command chair and the neuro-connectivity cables. As he walked toward one of the side viewing panels, he was thankful that Commander Kray had already clicked on opaque mode. Zak had great views from every angle within his Plate. He was taking in the three hundred and sixty-degree views of his surroundings as he hovered. Before he keyed "ON" his FGO to begin recording his observations, Zak spent the next few minutes walking around inside his Plate. He looked down, around, and up, taking in the wonders of this mysterious place. He knew he could not be seen inside of his Plate, but it wasn't long before he realized that his Plate's exterior surface (which was metallic gray) was beginning to attract unwanted attention.

Chapter 3

INTELLIGENT LIFE?

The objective of Zoom Convoy Missions, as with all missions, is to seek out intelligent life. Directors and TST's are to observe and document the presence of any intelligent life. If any intelligence is found, TST's are to attempt to communicate and confirm the existence and acceptance of the three positive principles, Peace, Love and Harmony. Through this communication, a closer bond will develop between all creatures in the Universe.

Zak walked over and grabbed his FGO from its holder. He clicked the toggle switch next to the holder to ON. The Plate's recording status was set to "ready." On the surface of his Orb, he felt for the rough spot that referenced the letters "Obs." He pressed the rough spot. The Orb's internal view changed from its previous 3D display of mission status, to expanding concentric circles, indicating "RECORDING". When the Orb was placed back into its holder, the Plate linked and reset all viewing ports to Record Mode. "RECORDING," his Plate announced in a pleasant audible voice.

Zak returned to viewing at another of the Plate's side Visual Panels. Looking down, he saw some creatures looking up and pointing at him, or rather pointing at his Plate.

"This is a NO, NO for efficient observations," he thought to himself. He knew that the observer must not be seen by the observed. Zak became alarmed as he noticed even more creatures

21

gathering down below looking up and pointing at his Plate.

TST's directing their Plates or ORBs were the designated communicators; they were sent specifically to communicate with creatures of other planets. Zak was not even qualified to attempt to communicate with these creatures. Zak intimated a command/thought that thirty-thousand feet would be a good distance to move away from this commotion. Zoom! Before he could even step away from his viewing panel, his Plate had repositioned to thirty-thousand feet and was hovering there.

"Whoa!" said Zak, this time out loud. "I have to remember I'm not neuro-connected." Zoom movements when standing unconnected can be dizzying, even to Directors. "In the chair. In the chair," he repeated to himself out loud as a reminder for the next time he intimated a "thought command". Looking again into his forward-looking monitor, he settled into his command chair. Zak decided to reposition into a thick bank of clouds over another city about one hundred and twenty miles from his current position.

With this thought command completed, Zoom! He was instantly hovering four thousand five hundred feet above another city within his quadrant, completely concealed within the cloud layer spread out above the city. All at once, Zak realized that he'd breached flight protocols twice. He'd used unauthorized speeds inside a Planetary atmosphere. He'd used Zoom speed twice, instead of Flash speed. Hoping that Commander Kray might have missed the infractions on his convoy monitor screen, or was too busy to notice a little speeding, Zak decided to resume his observations from this new location. Walking over and looking down toward the surface again, he saw many interesting things inside his clear glass bubble.

Zak wanted to avoid any more trouble. He decided to

disengage Zoom Speed by toggling OFF the Zoom OFF switch, located on the panel below his forward-looking monitor. He planned to verify if he had been recording, and if so, to delete the negative footage by resetting his Orb. He stepped away from the Visual Panel he was looking through, turned, and unfortunately only completed one of the two tasks. He walked over to his Command chair, leaned over, and checked to see if his FGO had been recording this whole time, which it was. He grabbed it, pressed the reset button to erase everything previously recorded, and pressed ON again to start recording a new observation session. He placed the Orb back into its holder but completely forgot to turn Zoom Speed OFF!

"Recording!" his Plate announced in a soft clear tone.

He walked back over to another Visual Panel and resumed his observations of what was going on down below. Zak observed the following sights:

• Small four-legged creatures walking in front of and leading larger two-legged creatures with a rope.

• Two-legged creatures sitting in groups, appearing to be eating.

• Many machines with creatures inside, moving in parallel patterns on roadways near the walking two-legged creatures. During these observations, Zak's eyes would follow a group of either walking or flying creatures. His Plate would subtly and silently track moving along with his eye movement to keep the targets clearly visible.

• There were two-legged creatures riding on the backs of other larger four-legged creatures.

• Large groups of two-legged creatures separated by green spaces, waving, and appearing to be cheering about the small group of creatures running on a green space.

• All sizes of four-legged creatures seemed to drop something from behind them onto the surface and the two-legged creatures would either pick it up and place it into bags or scoop it up and place it into containers.

Zak was concentrating on observing his targets down below. Although he was within a cloud bank at four thousand five hundred feet, there was a high level of detail upon or surrounding his targets when viewing through any one of the crafts visual beam portals. "BEEP, BEEP, BEEP. Drifting, Drifting," his Plate announced pleasantly. The audible prompting from his Plate indicated that he needed to check his forward-looking display monitor. Using the monitor would give him the "Materialized View" of his situation.

Zak looked at the real-world view of his Plate on the Monitor. In contrast to the cloud bank, which was now above and behind his Plate, it indicated that his Plate was now clearly visible to all observers. "BEEP, BEEP, BEEP. Drifting, Drifting," his Plate pleasantly announced again. He was still drifting away from his concealment. As Zak stepped over to his Command Chair in preparation to relocate to yet another position, a very loud alarm sounded.

"DANGER! DANGER! DANGER!" his Plate announced, this time with urgency! Horrified, Zak glanced at his forward-looking monitor. Three military jet aircrafts were screaming toward his location

Chapter 4

THE CHASE

Zak looked around, within, and through his Visible Panels to the outside surroundings of his current position. He was aware that he had drifted a significant distance from where he had started his observations. He was still hovering in obscure opaque mode and still at four thousand five hundred feet above ground level. He had in fact, drifted outside of his cloud bank covering due to his subconscious Plate maneuverings.

"Flush!" Zak said out loud. "I think I really messed up this time." Zak saw the jets approaching from his southwest position at three thousand feet and climbing.

"DANGER, DANGER, DANGER!" Zak's Plate warned with urgency. The lighting of the entire internal space was transformed to "Blinking Red." Zak strapped himself to his Command Chair. "DANGER..." before the third alert sounded, he quickly shut off the alerts with a thought and leaned back into his Command chair placing his right hand onto his control pad.

Zak's Plate immediately switched to luminous visibility and flashed one brilliant burst of light as it began to slowly move away from the chasing crafts. He then intimated a speed matching evasive maneuver keeping himself in front of the approaching aircrafts.

Zak saw the yellow lines popping up on his monitor for one, two and then three radar locks onto his Plate. He decided to remain engaged for a bit as he led the jets in a circular pattern up to eighteen thousand feet (with a cautionary thought to jam any threat that was posed by them, like putting on gloves when handling Bee's or Wasp's). The jets finally arrived at eighteen thousand feet, which to Zak, seemed like a very long and slow climb. He noted on his monitor that the climbing speeds registered at Mach 2.4 or 1,841 miles-per-hour. Now that everyone was speeding along at eighteen thousand feet, Zak decided to leave them there for a while. Back to four thousand five hundred feet he intimated. Zoom! Zak's Plate instantly resumed its hover at four thousand five hundred feet to the same spot where he'd first been observed by the jets.

Zak's Monitor showed the jets had broken formation and were searching for their previous radar target locks. Zak laughed to himself as he was observing his monitor. The jets searching radar detector images reaching out but not responding to anything appeared like little ants wobbling about holding onto long pieces of spaghetti.

Zoom! Instantly there were two Plates hovering at four thousand five hundred feet. "How's it going with your observations here Zak?" asked Commander Kray, who'd just appeared in hover next to Zak's Plate.

"Uhh, uhh, fine," said Zak, afraid that everything he'd just done had been observed by his Commander.

Zak's Orb was still in record mode. The reality was even worse than his fear, all of Zak's actions had been streamed LIVE on video back to GREY3110227 DPF Administration. "I don't think so Director!" his commander responded. "It doesn't look like things are fine at all, right here, right now. You've compromised this whole Quadrant, so prepare for repositioning. And for goodness' sake, turn OFF your Zoom Speed button, now!"

"Yes, Sir, will do," Zak replied.

"Stand by while I get your new position coordinates!" the Commander barked. Zak unstrapped himself from his chair, leaned out and pressed the Zoom Speed toggle switch down for OFF. The Zoom indicator light went out. He leaned back into his Command chair, strapped back in, and awaited further orders.

"I can't believe I didn't do that earlier," Zak zested to himself in disgust.

He knew he wasn't authorized to do what he had done. All he could do was to sit and wait until his commander decided to either demand he turn OFF his NSD Control for repositioning, or allow Zak to leave his NSD Control ON, so that he could fly himself to the pending repositioned coordinates. He knew being repositioned by the Commander, was akin to a total lack of faith that Zak could follow basic orders. The best he could hope for was that he'd be allowed to independently either fly or Flash to the new location. As Zak stood/sat into his command chair just waiting, with his right hand on his control stand, he could see that the jets were in a screaming return down to their current elevation.

"DANGER, DANGER, DANGER!" Zak's Plate warned with urgency! The beeping alerts had returned inside the Plate, indicating that he and the Commander were both potentially becoming targets. "DANGER, DANGER, DANGER!" Zak's Plate warned. Sounds were bouncing all around and echoing from within his craft and inside his head, as he could hear his alarms being echoed into Commander Kray's craft. Zak was distraught. He was very conscious of the fact that his commander was hearing the distress alarms coming from his Plate. Zak didn't dare think of disabling the warning alerts himself. He knew the Commander was hearing everything and could easily stop the noise if he desired. He just endured it.

"DANGER, DANGER, DANGER!" Zak's Plate warned again.

"Okay," crackled his commander into his consciousness. "I'm going to allow you to get out of this mess."

"DANGER, DA…"

"Hold on," the Commander instantly stopped the Plate's warning announcements. "As I was saying," the Commander continued, "I'm going to allow you to get out of this mess, but Zoom Speeds are in no way authorized down here, from now on, do you understand, Director?" the Commander barked.

"Yes, Sir, I do, Sir, thank you, Sir," said Zak.

"Okay, repeat these coordinates after me," his commander said, "W-Q-8-X-2-4-…"

As the Commander was calling out the coordinates verbally, Zak was typing and could see on his monitor that the Jets were passing through six thousand feet and leveling off for intercept with them at their current altitude of four thousand five hundred feet.

"3-7-H-2-5-0-0, now repeat!" the Commander barked.

"W-Q-8-X-2-4-3-7-H-2-5-0-0," repeated Zak audibly.

They both knew that this double work of thinking and speaking was used to lock Zak's Plate into the correct coordinates to fly as well. "Destination confirmed," audibly sounded inside Zak's Plate.

"I'll see you there," his Commander said.

And then, "FLASH!" the Commander was gone with one bright burst of light.

"DANGER, DANGER, DANGER!" Zak's Plate began to alert once again with urgency; red blinking lights and all. The jets were now fifteen miles to Zak's North, in sight and closing. Zak, startled from his upbraiding, glanced back to his Monitor. He saw that the jets had locked onto his Plate. The threat signature on his monitor clicked from yellow to RED Alert Status. "DANGER, DANGER, DANGER!" his Plate warned, followed by, "BEEP! BEEP!"

"Jam!" Zak intimated as a command to his Plate. He knew the jets were clicked over to "HOT" on their anti-aircraft missiles. "Let's Go!" was the next thought command! His Plate flashed one resplendent burst of light, like a brilliant star and began to move away from the jets (which were now one and a half miles away, clearly visible, and in attack posture.)

Zak's Plate departed instantly, matching and assuming the jets speed and maintaining a one and a half mile distance between them. While initiating stand by for his Plate's rear facing target jamming defense, Zak's finger hovered over the "EMT" button, and lightly tapped it. "Plate shield activated." This time the Plate used a soft re-assuring voice. Should any of the jets select any type of weaponry to fire upon Zak, their actions would become ineffective and non-responsive to the pilots' commands and control.

"Flash to destination please," Zak intimated. FLASH! With one brilliant burst of light, gone.

As Zak's Plate was flashing to his new location, he was enjoying the views he observed looking through his Plate's interior, through its Visible Panels to the outside surroundings as the landscape moved under and around him in a dizzying display of colors and contours. Instinctively Zak clicked OFF his View Panels, to eliminate the kaleidoscopic whirlwind of colors bouncing throughout his Plate. Soon, his Plate slowed, and stopped. He had arrived.

Upon destination arrival, Zak's Plate vocally confirmed the

following: "W-Q-8-X-2-4-3-7- H-2-5-0-0. Destination confirmed!"

Zak could see on his forward-looking monitor that his Plate was hovering slightly below his Commander's one o'clock position. "Okay, you've had your fun, Director!" his Commander stated. "Now, reset your "Obs" and try to do a better job here, of concealing your observations from Humans."

"Yes, Sir, will do, Commander, Sir," Zak replied. FLASH! The Commander was gone.

As Zak was unstrapping himself from his command chair, he wondered what on GREY his commander was talking about when he mentioned "Humans." Zak had never heard that term before.

"Well, anyway, I'm in a different location, with a new start, so, things are looking up," he thought. He grabbed his Orb, reset it to "Obs," and replaced it into its holder.

"RECORDING," his Plate announced in a pleasant audible voice. He walked over to his monitor to observe his surroundings before he clicked back ON his outward looking View Panels to begin his observations at this new location.

Chapter 5

DIFFERENT CREATURES

Zak clicked "ON" on his View Panels, and immediately discovered he was completely surrounded by either water or sky. He was now hovering over an ocean, with clear skies above, stationary at five hundred feet above the water. Zak was more curious now than he'd ever been. Knowing he was in a completely different part of this Planet (and secure in the fact that he wasn't going to be seeing any ants carrying spaghetti on his forward-looking monitor any time soon) he walked over to yet another of his Visual Panels and gazed down. Above surfaces like water, the Plates Visual Panels only allowed Zak to see clearly down to about twenty feet below the surface. He was only able to make out some shadowy movements below that. He walked over to one of the six Visual Beam Portal monitors, leaned down onto it, and began to adjust the lighting.

The Portal's Beam, when set to the right frequency and intensity easily identified and magnified the strata of the ocean depths. Everything within the light of the portal monitor appeared to be flying in mid-air throughout the depths of the ocean. Scanning left, right, and all around he saw millions of creatures of all sizes, shapes, and colors flying at various depths in all directions. Even the creatures on the very bottom were climbing in and out of holes and rocks, way down (from this vantage point) on what looked like the ground level of the Planet. Zak began to wonder about the other Directors on this mission. How were they faring with their observations?

"As NSD's," he reflected, "Our job is to search for intelligent creatures so that the TST's can follow up and impart our message of Peace, Love and Harmony." Zak knew they had completed many successful missions throughout the universe, but this Blue Planet was going to be a challenge. "None of these creatures appear to know how to greet and welcome visitors," Zak said aloud as it was too baffling a thought to keep in his head.

Zak was preparing to intimate a new command, repositioning to a depth below the surface, when his Plate sounded an alert, "ATTENTION, ZOOM MISSION CONVOY! ATTENTION, ZOOM MISSION CONVOY! Begin to wrap up your observations. You will be contacted to terminate your observations in thirty minutes. Over," came the neuro-communications from Commander Kray.

"Wow, I've lost a lot of time on this mission. I bet that my mission here and my mission channel at home will immediately be deleted, if DPFA even allows anyone to view it," Zak thought regretfully. "Well, I still have a few more minutes," he thought. So, he decided to go ahead and reposition to a depth of fifteen hundred feet below the surface.

He was standing and viewing down through the Visual Beam Portal's monitor when his Plate tilted to a forty-five-degree angle and flashed down to a hover at fifteen hundred feet below the water's surface. Because of the speed in which his Plate Flashed to its destination depth, Zak couldn't get very clear views of any of the creatures he saw flying past his Port Beam viewers. Zak still marveled at all the sights. He had never been in an area with so many flying creatures. Above, below, and all around his Plate were creatures of every shape, size, and color. This time, Zak intimated for his Plate to move very, very slowly. He turned on all Visual Beam Portal Lights, capturing stunning visual images of this phase of his observations. His Plate began to slowly cruise through the ocean, its six portal lights illuminating the depths in rotating patterns as they moved. Although only TST's were tasked with communicating to intelligent creatures of other Planets, Zak knew how to identify intelligence when it was found. In addition to their acceptance of the principles of Peace, Love and Harmony (which are gifts delivered by means of telepathy). It is well known that intelligent creatures and beings are desirous of highly intelligent communications. They have a clear and specific way of expressing their willingness to the presenters of such gifts; it's all done through telepathy, producing raw truth. No interpretations necessary.

Zak thought his neuro-connective communications had been statically interrupted when his Plate was surrounded by a large group of flying creatures with blunt pointy noses. He observed these creatures flying all around his Plate and attempting to rub their bodies against the outer shell in an odd manner. They were twisting and twirling, rolling over and over in a seemingly playful manner, indicating that they wanted to climb aboard and chat. They were clicking and squeaking and making lots of noise.

This was a very peculiar experience for Zak. He had only heard about this type of thing happening to other TST's on missions. Other convoy's observation videos, and communications had been received back home by the Authorities at DPFA. Based on the content of the videos, they would assign TST's to follow-up on any observations that showed intelligence. Zak thought he had observed his first intelligent creatures. But he didn't know for sure.

"ATTENTION, ATTENTION! One minute to complete observations. Over," came the neuro-command from

Commander Kray. Startled out of his trance observing the beauty of these wonderful looking creatures, Zak hurried to his command chair, strapped himself in and pressed his "Obs" button to turn OFF his official task of recording Planet Blue Observations. He placed his right hand onto his control pad. Yikes! He realized that he'd forgotten to turn off his six Visual Beam Portal lights which were continuing their scan of the ocean in a disco ball random circling pattern.

Just as he was wondering if he had enough time to step out of his command chair to disengage the lights, Commander Kray's voice loudly crackled into his neuro-communications link, "ATTENTION, ATTENTION! ZOOM MISSION CONVOY! On my mark, prepare to turn off your NSD controls for repositioning. Press your buttons… NOW!"

"NSD Control De-Activated," announced Zak's Plate firmly. Zoom! Zak's Plate complied as commanded and instantly displayed Zak's Plate along with the other forty-nine Plates, repositioned eighty miles above Planet Blue's surface. Their orientation was pointing straight down, with the planet now at their backs, or above them as they were all facing downward toward the dark open outer space.

Right in front of him, floating in the space between himself and his display monitor, was the 3D depiction of Planet Blue at the top region of space, with another smaller planet up and to its left. The fifty Plates were aligned below the Blue Planet in a multiple diamond formation. The Plates' formation combined to form the appearance of an arrowhead that was pointing straight down from the planet. Commander Kray's Plate was at the tip of the lowest point of the formation.

Zak had to shake his head for clarity as he looked at the 3D image in the space before him. It was depicting their pre-Zoom flight positioning, but something appeared to be wrong. He saw what he thought was his Plate, in the middle, outer left side of the diamond formation with its lights twirling around. The formation was tight, except for Zak's Plate, which was looking more like a party ball on New Year's Eve, rather than a serious planet hopping interstellar space craft. All crafts were white in color except Zak's, which was indicating Red. "Could you please extinguish those flood lights Xason Zong!" his Commander barked, into the open communications line which was audible within all Plates.

Embarrassed, and humbled to hear his Commander call him by his given name, Zak disconnected himself from his command chair, stepped forward to below his forward-looking monitor and depressed the button marked "VBP-A", to shut off all Visual Beam Portal lights at once. The button's light confirmed OFF when it went out. Zak stepped back into his command chair, replaced his right hand onto his control pad, and thankfully noticed the absence of the previous light show display on his floating 3D image.

He saw that the multi-diamond formation of Plates that were originally white, were now all blinking yellow. "Prepare for departure." Commander Kray intimated to all Mission Crafts. Zak observed the mission fleet switch colors again from blinking yellow to green, still pointing straight down. "Can we proceed with the conclusion of our mission, Director Zong?" His commander asked. Again, on "Open Mike," as it were.

"Yes, Sir. Please, Sir," Zak intimated in reply.

Chapter 6

BACK HOME

"Stand by," Commander Kray said calmly. Zak could hear the other Directors laughing and finding humor in his "lights issue" mistake. On the other hand, he was pleased to hear the Commander's voice was calmer than it had been. Plus, he did call him a director, which Zak was always proud to hear from anyone, especially his commanding officer. Zak fixed his gaze on the orientation of the Plates. It was not obvious to him when they arrived at this planet, that it was positioned straight up from their own GREY planet. He only knew that in open space there is no up, nor down nor backward. Every flight pattern he'd ever seen or even thought of, was always aimed either straight up, or due east or west. Never out and down, or in this case, straight down.

There was an extremely bright flash of light that emanated from the entire group of Plates. Zoom! They were gone. Planet Blue was no longer visible in front of him. Zak loved the enroute portion of Zoom Mission Convoys. Even though total control of the fleet was in the hands of Commanders, he enjoyed that they never took too long, because commanders could easily extend or shorten a trip on a whim using unlimited Zoom Speed Authorizations. He had mixed feelings about this particular mission though.

He was happy about his encounter with the creatures of the ocean, but unhappy about his unauthorized use of Zoom speeds, being seen by radar probing Jets, and obviously, the lights incident. Other than that, he was happy to see Planet Blue fading behind them (or above them given his continuing disorientation). Zak got excited as their green target line, which connected them to GREY3110227 began to unwind from its crooked transition phase to a mad dashing straight line home.

"ATTENTION, ATTENTION! PREPARE FOR ZOOM DISINGAGEMENT!" came the announcement from Commander Kray's craft. Again, as always, just when it seemed by their approach speed that they'd get impaled by their own planet, they started to slow down. Zak always thought coming out of Zoom speed felt very cool as the anti-gravity brakes assisted in slowing.

The convoy patterns began to shift from enroute diamond formation back to the familiar home bound string line formation for the descent back onto the Departure Deck Pads. Once all Plates transitioned inside their planet's atmosphere, the Zoom Mission Convoy Plates Flashed, with one burst of bright light to their positions sixty feet above their stations, and in unison began their slow descent onto their pads. Commander Kray switched all crafts forward-looking monitors from mission flight visuals to a picture of himself. "Good job, Directors, I've already heard from DPF Administration that they're very happy with some of the observations we made on this mission. Welcome home. That is all."

The Monitor screens went blank, and all neuro-connectivity ties began automatically disengaging and retracting. Zak's formerly impermeable Plate was immediately breached by Jay as he walked up the ramp into the heart of the craft. He said with excitement, "Welcome home, Sir, everyone is so excited about your observation's, Sir."

"Thanks, Jay," said Zak as he unbuckled and stepped out of

his command chair. "Commander Kray just mentioned that we all did a good job," he said glibly. Zak reached over and grabbed his FGO from its holder and took a step toward the ramp.

Jay said, "No, no, Sir, I said your observations, the ones you took in this Plate, Sir."

"What?" said Zak, confused. "I don't understand."

Before Jay could clarify, up the ramp ran Zing, Zak's brother who leapt up and knocked his brother back into his Command Chair. "K! you're amazing! You've done it. You have done it!" exclaimed Zing.

"Done what, G?" shoving his brother off him so he could stand up again.

"Made a discovery!" Zing and Jay said in unison.

"A what?" asked Zak.

"A discovery, a discovery. Your observation was released immediately by DPFA before it was screened and scheduled for viewing later. Most greys have already seen your awesome images. It's created a major buzz across the whole planet, K!" Zing said.

"Wow," Zak thought. He had absolutely no idea what the flush Zing and Jay were talking about. He felt dizzy trying to understand what they had just told him, when up the ramp walked Commander Kray.

Zak immediately stood to attention, and Zing and Jay stepped back and away from Zak. "Director!" exclaimed Commander Kray. "You're gonna need to come with me, young grey."

"Yes, Sir," Zak replied, as Commander Kray turned and walked down the ramp. Zak held his hands up with an inquisitive look like, "What the flush is going on?" to his brother and Jay as he followed Commander Kray.

Zak stepped out onto the departure deck following the Commander and found himself walking in stride with Gary Sparkz, TST, who had just arrived back from his own separate mission to Planet 5. Gary had overheard from other Planet Blue Directors about Zak's little experience on Planet Blue. As fate would have it, he ended up walking in step right next to Zak who was following Commander Kray.

Gary took this opportunity to whisper to him, "Listen, Zak, don't take the beating you're about to receive too hard. Old man Kray will tell ya it's just to make a better Director out of ya. Good luck!" he said as he turned onto the post mission walkway toward the lockers and showers.

Chapter 7

DISCOVERY CHANNELS

Commander Kray walked ahead of Zak on the Mission Departure Dock silently. Just beyond the pre-flight shower exit doors was the DPF Admin door. The Commander opened the door and entered. The sign above the door read... "DEPARTURE PREPARATION FACILITY ADMINISTRATION". Zak caught the door before it closed, entered, and turned left following Commander Kray down the hallway.

The Commander's office was right across the hall from the Craft Assignment Desk (CAD), for Plate and ORB craft logouts. CAD was also the location to drop off post-mission Flight Guide Orbs for data dumping of their Obs videos. There they would be downloaded, cleaned, and scrubbed to be readied for the next Craft Logouts or authorized Convoy Mission use. After every Mission, all Directors and TST's must drop off their FGO's at the CAD.

Zak was still following Commander Kray toward his office. He wanted to hold onto his FGO because if he got fired, at least he'd be able to sign it back in as his last official act as a director. He was just hoping, no matter what Zing and Jay said, that he wasn't in serious trouble. As the Commander entered his office to the left, without turning around, he told Zak, "Drop your FGO at the counter and come on in."

"Oh man, that's not good," Zak thought to himself. "I can't even sign it back in." Zak dutifully dropped his FGO on the counter and didn't even notice that every CAD attendant was looking at him smiling.

The Commander closed the door after Zak entered. "Have a seat, Director," Commander Kray said as he walked around to sit in his larger chair. Zak pensively took the seat facing the Commander's desk. "I won't keep you Zak, but I wanted to personally tell you what a good job you did capturing those Dolphin videos and comments back on Blue."

"Again, with the weird words!" Zak thought to himself. "When, and where, were these things I caught?" Zak thought consciously.

"Just before we left the Planet," his commander replied in response to Zak's conscious thought. Shocked at what he'd just heard, Zak froze. In zest mode, Zak thought, "What's a Dolphin?"

"What comments?" And did he just hear his commander actually call him by his "pet name"?

After what seemed like twenty minutes, Zak replied, "ah, well ah…"

"Listen, Zak, I know I was hard on you back on Blue, but I have to set an example for the other Directors," the Commander said. "We are always striving for excellence. I'll need you to tighten up your concentration when we're in the field next time. Your two major negative marks, blowing your cover and getting tracked on radar are bad enough, but you cannot go around and over these planets Zooming in and out of existence," he continued. "It freaks these creatures out. It's hard enough for the TST's to get close to them without them being afraid by our near dimensional shifting speeds. I know you'll do better next time. Won't you?" he asked.

"Yes, Sir, I will," Zak responded, still very confused about what was going on.

"Listen," said his commander, "you're going to be presented with a Presidential Medal tomorrow, by President Quay for your Obs video captures from today." The Commander looked at Zak (who was still frozen in shock) he could see that he was talking to a full vessel. "I can see from your face that you're gonna need time to get some rest. Also, you will want to have some time to view the telecasts of your "Discovery Channel."

"It's being broadcast on a continuous loop because of its significance to our planet's overall Mission." The Commander rose from his seat and said, "Okay, you're dismissed, Director. Go hit the showers, get some grub and a little viewing in before a good night's sleep. You'll need to be back here tomorrow afternoon for the presentation. I believe the President will be sending an ORB to get you, so get on up out of here, Director."

"Yes, Sir," Zak said as he rose to leave.

The last comments didn't even register as Zak was so overwhelmed. His head was spinning so hard he actually felt blood rushing to his head to keep him conscious as he stood up. He shook the Commander's hand and turned to leave his office. Zak was dizzier than he'd ever been, even during his most complex Plate maneuver training exercises as a pre-Director, years ago. He walked unsteadily past the CAD again to silent admiring stares, out the DPF Admin door and down the departure dock past the pre-flight shower exit doors.

He only fully came to his senses as he was turning left off the dock and onto the Post Mission Entrance toward the lockers and showers. "What the flush was the Commander talking about," he thought. Zak showered, feeling like he was the only person in the building, although there were other Directors still dressing or talking and cavorting all around him. When he exited the DPF building, he was pleased to see G still hanging around the communal area waiting for him.

"K!" Zing exclaimed as he headed toward his brother. "You ready to go home and have something to eat?"

"Yeah, I can't tell you how confused I am right now," Zak said.

"I'll bet," Zing said. "Betty told me to tell you to expect to be picked up by an ORB tomorrow morning at 9:00 a.m. sharp. And, she said I could come along too, so how sprayed is that? Huh? Huh?"

"Pretty waxed I guess," Zak said, returning from the lingering brain fog from his earlier conversation with the Commander. Neither brother had ever ridden in an ORB before. Zak hadn't even considered training to become a TST because you need total dedication, body, mind, and soul, to the missions.

Tomorrow was gonna be a great experience. He hoped his head would be clear by then. He'd heard that ORB travel was an order of magnitude greater than Plate travel, so it was sure to be mind-blowing.

As they left the DPF Building grounds, Zing said, "Ah, don't worry, K, it'll all make sense soon enough. I already have our viewers at home set to your Discovery Channel."

Chapter 8

THE VIEWING

Zak and Zing had a short night. As they ate dinner, Zak was amazed at the descriptive platitudes sent his way for capturing the unprompted pleadings from the Dolphins on Planet Blue. Both Zak and Zing became educated about the Blue Planet which they later discovered was called Earth. Zing learned about Dolphin's from watching TST ORB video observation captures. He even learned about "Humans" from time to time on various Discovery Channels.

Zak was not a big viewer watcher. He was either on missions or studying. He hardly ever had time to watch his own Discovery Channel. Zing explained to Zak, "The DPF Administration had found (over the thousands of years of mission work) that TST's teleported creatures including humans. When placed before certain objects or other creatures from their own planets, they exude sounds. With the aid of the DPFA 's Engineering team, the TST's have been able to interpret those sounds to be methods of communication to describe other creatures in their respective languages. This has been true even for the blue Planet, Earth.

"That's how we knew "Your" creatures were called Dolphins!" Zing informed his brother. "And it's how we'll learn their "Terminology" someday, from these Discovery Channels. We've done the same thing I hear with Whales, Dolphins, Orangutans and even the lone Pyrenean Ibex that we brought here as the very last survivor of his kind from Planet Blue," said Zing.

"But until they heard the Dolphins speaking on Discovery Channel — "Xason Zong," they never really understood what they were trying to convey. The TST's couldn't believe the pain of their words, in comparison to the look of joy and happiness they displayed in their faces and movements. They didn't want to play; they were frantically pleading for HELP! They wanted to be taken from Earth. They were saying that the Blue Planet was dying, and they wanted to go where there was Love, Peace, and Harmony! The magic words that were sought throughout the Universe. Finally, Intelligent Life!"

On and on the education went until Zing and Zak fell asleep. Early the next morning Zing communicated the reminder message from Betty, for Zak to be ready for transport to DPF promptly at 9:00 a.m. There was going to be a celebration for him to be recognized for his recent observations.

At the appointed time, both Zak and Zing were waiting outside their home quarters when they saw a bright light appear over the horizon. As it got closer, it transitioned from a glowing light into a liquid metal looking ORB of brilliant shining light against the morning sky. It came silently gliding over the mountain ridge, foothills, and fields from the east. It grew in size without making a sound as it approached and came to a hover about forty feet above and in front of where they were standing. They stood there looking up at it when a beam of green light engulfed them both. They felt their bodies being lifted toward the ORB. Once the green light lifted them into the ORB, they were then engulfed in white light as they hovered above the interior floor within the craft. They both felt as if they were being wrapped in a soft white blanket.

A neighbor started to yell, "Have a good day!" but he was too late. Zap! A brilliant burst of light, and then, gone.

The ORB Zapped and brilliantly appeared above one of the DPF ORB docking stations. When it had descended to three feet above ground, it rematerialized from a lit ball of glowing brilliance to become a metallic orb with an opened door, out of which Zak and Zing easily stepped out onto the departure deck.

Commander Kray saw them arrive and walked over to greet them. He held out his hand, shook Zings hand, then grabbed Zak's shoulder and said, "Follow me, honored guest."

Outside of the DPF Admin building were Zak's fellow Planet Blue Convoy Directors and TST's. They were all being instructed to enter the building. Zing was instructed to follow the Directors in and sit with them during the proceedings.

Commander Kray held the door open for Zak. "After you, Director," Commander Kray said. Zak entered the doorway and began climbing the stairs to the second floor. All he really knew was that some kind of presentation was going to be made to him. Why? He still wasn't sure. Up on the second floor landing, he continued walking down another long corridor with double glass doors at the end. Zak could hear footsteps ahead of them from the forty-eight other pilots and Zing.

"This way, gentlegreys," said a secretary instructing the group ahead of them.

From behind they saw some other double doors open down the left side hallway. Zak also heard the secretary announce inside the room, "Here they are, Mr. President!" as she stepped aside allowing the train of Directors, TST's, Zing, Zack, and the Commander into the room.

Chapter 9

THE HUMAN

"Congratulations, gentlegreys! We are all very proud greys today. I am speaking for the entire planet," said President Uda Quay, the leader of Planetary Expeditions for Intelligent Life (PEIL) for the DPFA. "This day is going to be remembered forever," the President said, as he was welcoming the guests and suggesting they find a seat at one of the many tables in the conference room.

Zak was introduced to the President by Commander Kray. He just stood there, stunned as the President reached down and grabbed his hand and shook it vigorously. The President excused both himself and Zak from the Commander and escorted Zak up front to his seat beside him at the head table. Before he sat down, President Uda Quay thanked everyone for attending this special session. He motioned for the lights to be turned down as he took his seat.

Four huge screens descended from the ceiling. The room went from dark to light as all four screens reflected the still image of Zak's Obs's initial observation frames. To the surprise and shock of everyone (except the President, and his aides who were stationed throughout the room) a spotlight was turned on in the center of the room. Standing there in front of them was a large, pale colored, giant of a creature. The creature was wearing a voice conversion mask to convert its vocalizations into a language the greys could understand.

"Hello, my name is John Baker. I'm forty-six years old. I'm a single male, never married. I'm from Amboy, Washington, United States of America, North American Continent, The Blue Planet — Earth. I understand your planet's mission, and I agree with it. I'm also thankful to be able to help your cause. I've been seeking Peace, Love and Harmony my whole life.

"I was just standing on a hill one day six years ago. We had smoke all around us from the fires that were burning in California, Oregon, and Washington. I had my arms upstretched and was asking the Lord for some breathable air to relieve the choking fumes from the forest fires and for the safety of our fire fighters. I was prompted to open my eyes and look up. Which I did. I looked almost straight up over my head to see a bright round glowing ball of light in the sky shining right over my head.

"It kinda freaked me out 'cause it was silent, just hovering there, shining beautifully. I didn't hear any words or anything, but I felt that ball asking my brain if I was an intelligent creature? In my mind, I thought well yeah, I think I am." Light amounts of laughter rippled through the room. "So, I said yeah in my brain." A little more laughter. "Then the light asked me if I would be willing to accept Peace, Love and Harmony in all of my future interactions with my fellow creatures on my planet? Again, I said yeah, I'd sure try. Then I heard it ask my brain, 'Would you be willing to help us in our mission to save your planet from the destructions that are going on here?'

"'Well, I guess I would,' I thought. I didn't know if I told my brain that though." Much more laughter broke out, because on Planet GREY3110227 communication was almost exclusively done by thought and intimations, rarely with speaking. So, it was funny to the group to hear him say that his thoughts and his brains were different beings. "Right then, I saw that bright ball blink a flash of white light, then next all I could see was green in my eyes." This time only the two TST's snickered. They are the ones that can Teleport with their beams. Sean is the TST that retrieved John on the recent Zoom Mission Convoy to Blue, and Shay who was also on the Mission, had retrieved Zak and Zing from their home for the meeting today.

"My first visit to your planet was six years ago. I'm happy to have been invited back here a second time. The first time I was here I think we established an understanding that we're not that different, except y'all are short purple fellas and we're big, not so bright folks, that think we're the smartest creatures in the Universe. Well, I for one know different. Thanks for inviting me back here. I loved the ride." This time there was a healthy round of applause from the entire congregation.

"I just want to say," John continued, "I was brought here this time in a real flying saucer." Light chuckles from Sean and Shay. "I was walkin' out of the Amboy Market yesterday, and right there in the sky was this metallic saucer looking thing, I hear y'all call 'em Plates. I knew it had to be you fellas when I heard it ask my brain if I could help y'all again. Well, I know I freaked out the folks at the store, 'cause I just set my groceries down right there on the ground and then just stood there lookin' up till the green light hit me." This time loud applause and laughter erupted in the meeting.

"So, lastly, I'd just like to thank my pilot, I think he's called Sean TST. Thank you, Sean. I see ya sitting out over there. Your President, Uda Quay has asked me to help y'all understand some things you don't quite understand, so bring it on. That's why I'm here. I'm ready when you are."

After a little rustling, the lights dimmed above John Baker. He sat on a stool in the middle of the room holding a Laser

Pointer. Zak's observation video began to roll on all four screens simultaneously depicting the static picture of a city street scene on Earth. Both Zak and Zing were still in disbelief that they were here, sitting in this room, on their own GREY Planet, with a Planet Blue creature.

A calm voice from the overhead speakers began to speak to the room. "Thank you, John, for being here with us again. Let's proceed with today's questions, shall we?"

"What?" thought Zak in zest mode. "These types of meetings have been going on before; with aliens from different Planets?" He looked around and saw other Directors equally astonished at what they'd just heard. Commander Kray was calmly reaching for his pen to take notes. Zing's mouth was wide open, and he was staring at the human.

"Now John, what are the small 4-legged creatures there on the street?" the voice from the ceiling asked. "Those small ones are called dogs. They are our pets which we humans keep for companionship and for huntin'," John replied.

"Your kind keep other creatures for companionship? This seems odd to us," said the voice.

"We keep all kinds of other creatures as companions. Cats, birds from the air, fish from the lakes and even horses which are much bigger than us humans," John said.

"Doesn't your kind believe that all creatures should be free? And that keeping them as pets takes away their freedoms?" the voice continued.

"We've done this for so long, we even think they like to be our pets," John replied.

"We cannot fix the past John; we're trying to fix the future. Perhaps you should stop making pets out of creatures that we should mutually respect," the voice said. "Next Question, what are the movement vehicles you humans are traveling about within?"

"Those we call cars and trucks. They help us to get around on our planet faster," John said proudly.

"Do they fly, John?" the voice inquired.

"Ha, Ha, Nope, not yet anyway. I think we're trying to make some that'll fly someday," said John.

"Remember to restrict their airspeeds for planetary movements John," the voice said. The whole room burst out into laughter. Remembering Zak's speeding issues on Earth. Zak put his head down on the table. Zing was smiling, but he didn't know why.

The voice went on, "We have a young Pilot here John, who had an incident of over speeding on your planet recently. So, you see, even we try to observe some courtesies when we travel." More laughter and pats on Zak's back.

John said, "Well, we also have jets and rockets on our planet that fly really, really fast."

"Yes John," the voice said, "we know about those crafts, as well as your missiles, bombs, and nuclear weapons. However, those items are topics for a different discussion in another forum."

"I hope y'all can help us stop hating each other and killing our planet," John said sadly.

"Our missions have been going on for thousands of years John, and we are finding intelligent life throughout the Universe. However, we've found that at times and for certain planets, we cannot help them, because they have too much hatred in their hearts. We're not sure if your planet is yet another that we cannot save," the voice said.

"Last question, on this section of the observation video.

What are the dogs dropping that your humans are picking up and placing in bags?"

"That's their poop. Or what I believe you all here call flushing's," John blushed.

"Eww!" everyone exclaimed groaning loudly within the room. "That's disgusting!" they all growled.

"John, you are aware that our missions are to seek out intelligent life, right?" the voice said. Again, boisterous laughter broke out.

"I'm sorry y'all," John said. "I just live there, I don't make the rules," he said with a smile. More laughs.

The lights came up and President Uda Quay rose to his feet to thank John for his assistance. "We will now be moving forward to the second phase of videos captured by our esteemed Director Xason Zong. But first, let us take a short fifteen-minute break, and we'll reconvene to review those videos next," said the President.

Chapter 10

SHORT BREAK

Out in the reception area of the DPFA building during break time, John Baker spotted Sean over against a far wall. He walked over to where Sean was standing. Approaching Sean, he knelt down so that he was almost at eye level with his Pilot. He reached out his hand to shake Sean's. The minute their hands touched, without Sean's lips moving, John heard Sean tell his brain, "It's such a pleasure to meet and know you, John. We're so happy to have you here with us today."

John let Sean's hand go, and said out loud, "Thank you, Sean, I'm glad to be here." Before he could stand up again, he noticed another hand being held out to him by Shay. He clasped Shay's hand and clearly heard Shay say, "Glad to meet you too John." Again without saying anything. John was amazed at this and continued to shake hand after hand with other greys that had formed a small line over against the wall to shake his hand and offer thanks.

In another area of the reception room Zak and Zing were standing close to each other and chatting. "Can you believe this flush?" Zak said to Zing.

Zing said, "I had no idea we were bringing aliens back here to our planet."

"Me neither," Zak said. "I knew that TST's had the ability to teleport for the study of various alien creatures. I never expected to meet one and have it talking with us, here on our own

Planet."

They both thought it was pretty freaky stuff. "I'm proud though," Zing said. "This makes me happy. It was a little weird at first but I'm warming to the idea of seeing and learning more about this Planet Blue, Earth." Zak just looked at his brother blankly. John truly admired the greys. He felt their love and humility and was receiving respect and admiration from all of them.

At the end of the short break, the President announced, "It's time to resume our guest presentations."

Chapter 11

THE DOLPHINS

After the break, the meeting attendees returned to the conference room to find it significantly changed. The four screens of viewing along with the four walls of tables and chairs had all been replaced by one very large screen at the back of the room, with eight rows of chairs facing the screen. After everyone had returned and was seated, President Uda Quay rose and stood in front of the big screen. "Again, many thanks to you all for your attendance on this most pivotal day for our planet and for the greys. Now, please just sit back and relax."

"Okay, Beth," he said as he walked over and sat back down next to Zak in the front row. The lights went down. Silently, the screen displayed Zak's Plate cruising through the ocean at fifteen hundred feet. The visual quality was stunningly sharp. The Plate's six Visual Beam Portal Lights were twirling and illuminating the depths of the ocean providing a stunningly beautiful display, showing all sizes, types, shapes, and colors of creatures, which appeared to be flying through space. At this point the video froze.

A different speaker's voice came on the overhead speakers. "Honorable President Quay, gentlegreys, Directors and guests. My name is Ooohhhh. I am a Whale." Loud gasps filled the hall. Murmurings were heard throughout the conference room.

"What the flush?" Zak thought as he looked over to his brother on the other side of the walkway. Zing was looking at

Zak with his mouth wide open and his eyes almost as big as the spots on his body.

OOOhhhh continued. "I am from a pod of six Gray Whales, out of the Pacific Ocean on planet Earth. Sean, your TST, coordinated the locating, extraction and transporting of me and my small pod here to your planet six years ago. My family and I are eternally grateful to Sean for saving us. I continue to be amazed, that I can speak to you all as I do.

"But I digress, forgive me," OOOhhhh said. "The video you have been viewing reminds me of how my family and I were found and saved. What you're about to see and hear, before the video goes black, is another intelligent family. They are Dolphins who are also pleading for their lives and to be taken away from Earth.

"Okay, I'm ready to begin…" The video began to roll again. Zak's Obs cameras are rolling and recording. "These creatures were observed flying all over his Plate and attempting to rub their bodies against its outer shell in what seemed to be a playful and loving manner. They were twisting and twirling, rolling over and over, indicating by their actions that they wanted to somehow climb aboard the craft. They were clicking and squeaking and making lots of noise," said OOOhhhh.

As the film rolled, OOOhhhh interpreted the pleadings from each of the Dolphin family members. "They are talking about the slaughter of their relatives and the pursuits they'd avoided and that of other Dolphins from other pods who were all being tracked and killed by humans, to use their bodies for food or to capture them and use them as pets. The older dolphins wanted to save their younger pod members and were pleading for this craft to take them."

Finally, right before the ship disappeared, the Dolphins were calling out that they wanted peace, love, and harmony with the humans. The room was silent. OOOhhhh's message had connected with every grey in attendance. As the screen went black, there was a brilliant flash of light. There was a slight pause, and the screen was raised.

The lights slowly went up in the room. There were noises and murmurs and stunned comments like, "I can't believe this. What the stars is that?" Wows, and jaw dropping awe, rippling through the room. There was lots of rustling. Chairs were moved out of the way as everyone was jockeying and crowding toward the front center of the room. What they were trying to see, which was now before them, lying in repose in a huge tank of sea water, with a telepathy band around its head, was Ooohhhh.

"Are there any questions from the audience," Ooohhhh asked, as he slightly bobbed his head. Everyone in the room either laughed or smiled in awestruck amazement.

"Ahh, I have a question," one of the Directors said. "How did you learn to talk and communicate?"

"All creatures and created beings communicate, at least within their own species. We've been communicating for thousands of years. But our species has had a very hard time living with Humans on Earth. They have had no desire to honor anything but our deaths. Only very recently have they stopped killing us in massive numbers and are just now beginning to see the intelligence that we possess."

"But more specifically to answer your question, engineers here in your facilities have created this head band, which allows me to understand each of you in my tongue, and you to understand me through my mind. The learning was instant. When I heard Sean's thoughts, and he heard mine. Instant communication," Ooohhhh said, bobbing his head up and down and splashing a bit of water from his tank. Applause and laughter for those getting wet who stood too near the tank.

"I also have a question, Ooohhhh," stated Sean. "When I prompted you through thought to stop swimming with your pod and come up to the surface and look up. What did you think when you saw my ORB?"

"Sean, that's an excellent question. I have never had a thought hit my brain like your request did. We also communicate in our pods with sounds and thoughts, but your communication, kind of shook me." Light laughter broke out. "I know, I get it. Me getting shook by Sean." More laughter and looks in Sean's direction. "But it did, and I don't know how or why. Anyway, I rolled on my side while still under water and saw a glimmer of your light. So, as pod leader, when I turned and began to surface toward it, the whole pod followed me. As I broke the surface, I'd never seen such a brilliant light so close. We were all amazed, and a little anxious. We had learned to be wary, due to Whaling boat lights."

"Do you remember what I asked you?" said Sean.

"Yes, absolutely," Ooohhhh said. "The words were the most beautiful words any creature of any planet can hear. You asked me if I was willing to accept Peace, Love and Harmony in all my future dealings with fellow creatures of my planet. And of course, I said yes, because I speak for my pod, and that's what all whales have been wanting for hundreds of years."

"So, thank you, Sean. You saved me and my pod. I know that your planet's mission is to save the whole of Planet Earth, and we all wish you success." Ooohhhh said with sincerity. Applause erupted throughout the room.

President Quay stepped a little forward and said, "Thank you very, very much, Ooohhhh. Your contribution to today's events has been more than any of us could have expected. We cherish you and welcome you and your family as life-long guests here on GREY if you choose to stay with us."

"Thank you, Mr. President, I will strongly consider your offer, Sir," said Ooohhhh.

"You're welcome, Ooohhhh," the President replied. Turning from Ooohhhh and facing the audience, the President said, "Remain standing everyone, we're almost done here."

"The Medal please," proclaimed the President to an attendant standing near a table with a box atop it. As the attendant was bringing the box to the President, the large screen to cover Ooohhhh's tank was lowered. "Again, don't bother being seated, unless you're tired, we have a short presentation to perform and then you'll all be dismissed."

The attendant stood to attention next to the President, holding a ribboned box, atop an ornate pillow. The President, waving his hand in the direction of John Baker, who was standing in the back row, said, "I would like to thank John Baker also for his fantastic contributions to today's educational events today." Lots of applause for John Baker. "Now, could Director Xason Zong please step forward." Zing had been standing next to his brother, who had somehow been shuffled back to midway inside the crowd that was viewing Ooohhhh's presentation.

"This is it, K!" Zing said, as he nudged his brother. Zak made his way to the front and stood before the President. The President motioned with his left arm for Zak to come stand next to him on his left.

"As President of the Departure Preparation Facility and Administration, and on behalf of our Planet GREY3110227, I mark this day in the annals of time as a key discovery for our greys." He turned to his right, unbound the golden medal, and lifted it from its box. Then he turned around to his left and instructed Zak to turn his back to him. He placed the gold necklace around Zak's neck, grabbed him by both shoulders and moved him forward and in front of him, proclaiming to the audience. "Here, greys, Directors, TST's, family and friends, is our latest planetary hero." Loud applause erupted. "You're all dismissed," proclaimed the President. Everyone took turns congratulating Zak, before heading to the exits.

Chapter 12

RINGS

After the gold medal presentation to Zak, congratulatory plaudits, hand shaking, and backslapping took place. On his way out of the conference room, Commander Kray made sure he made eye contact with both Sean and Shay to remind them of the meeting on RINGS tomorrow. "Yes, Sir," they both intimated, with an eyebrow raise. "We hadn't forgotten." They didn't need eye contact to hear the Commander's intimations, but it was an added personal touch of respect, extended to them both.

Of all the high level, hyper cool things TST's did, traveling to Planet Saturn (or RINGS as greys called it) for multi-universal meetings was a highlight for them. They got to reconnect with other planetary explorers and receive their very important bi-millennium instructions from ABOVE.

ABOVE, is where decisions are made regarding where to send Convoy Missions throughout the universe. This special meeting with these advanced super intelligent beings, was for the specific purpose of continuing and furthering the process of creating planetary and universal harmony. TSTs from GREY3110227 comprise just a few of the millions of Time and Space Travelers of the South Sector that were in the field seeking peace, love, and harmony.

While the rest of the presentation guests were leaving the meeting room, Zing was at his brother's side marveling at the bling Zak had just received from President Quay.

"Awesome, K!" said Zing, nudging his brother and grabbing the medal for closer inspection. "I'm gonna get me one of these someday," he said.

"Yeah, Sure you will," Zak thought. He was convinced it wasn't possible for his brother, who wasn't even on a path to become a Director.

"Hey! I heard that," Zing said.

"Oh, sorry, G, that negative thought just creeped through before I could Zest it. I apologize," Zak said. "I only meant, that your current educational training and pathway is along Plate and ORB Engineering and Craft Development. These pathways are typically "non-field" level expertise. Medals of this sort aren't typically awarded to engineers, is all," Zak further explained.

"I get it," said Zing understandingly, still wishing to himself that it was possible in some unforeseen way.

As they were exiting the conference room, both brothers glanced back toward the front of the room and saw Ooohhhh still inside his ocean water enclosed tank. He was rising silently, surrounded by green light emanating through the ceiling.

The next morning, the only visible sign that something big had been going on at the DPFA, was the absence of every single fleet ORB from the departure dock. All sixty ORBs were gone.

The planet Saturn, with its beautiful rings, was located within Earth's Solar System. It was the Universal Conference Center for the South Grey Sector of GREY3110227's Galaxy. The "Travelers" were continuing to add to the mass of participants, as they arrived and materialized into their pre-assigned pad locations on RINGS. Trams conveyed the Travelers directly to thousands of individual pad locations down from their Sky Port Docks at various entrances of the Huge Crystal Conference Center (C3) building. The Sky Port Docks and the

Conference Center were all housed within the expansive Hexagonal Globe of Space, which was fixed in perpetual hover fifteen miles below the torrentially swirling storms surrounding the planet, but not upon the planet's surface.

At the Port Docks and around each pad location, there was a very pleasant and continuous announcement, both lightly audible and subliminally broadcasted which repeated the message: "Welcome Travelers. thank you for coming." The message remained in each party's consciousness, until they began descending down and away from the docks and toward the Conference Center's entrances.

Zak and Zing made their way to their living quarters which had been pre-determined. Commander Kray and GREY's fifty-nine TST's quarters were located on floor 589 of the 700 floor Crystal Conference Center (C3). All quarters were spacious, accommodating, and plush by any standard. "All Travelers have from 8:00 a.m. to 2:30 p.m. to relax and prepare for the 3:00 p.m. to 6:00 p.m. meeting."

Commander Kray intimated to GREY Fleet, to bivouac or meet up at 2:00 p.m., at Hexagonal Landing 48 for a quick pre-meet before teleporting to their preassigned seats. To transform into translucent beings, then to transition back to your natural state is quite an extraordinary experience. The natural state of many Travelers may seem odd to all except the initiated (those beings who have traveled for many millenniums).

Sean, Shay and five other greys, showered their post transit gray flight coatings off their bodies returning them to their comfortable purple selves, yellow dots, and all. The seven of them chose to spend some time observing some of the other Travelers. They watched as some arrived for the meeting and saw some that had already shed their coatings and were moving around C3 in their natural states.

One of the group of seven was Gary Sparkz, TST. He was on his first mission to RINGS and looking forward to the experience. From their open balcony, they could see many wonderous sights through the massive expanse of space. As they looked down below, they noticed there was an even better place for sightseeing on Hexagonal Landing 4. So, down they all teleported. As they made their way to their open visualization zones, they found they were also being observed by other Travelers. There were very kind comments being intimated toward them about their natural states of appearances. This flattery was unexpected yet very much appreciated.

They each took up viewing positions and began the wonderous experience of observing the comings and goings of their fellow Travelers. Time and Space Travelers (TST), holding an invitation from "ABOVE" were the only beings that were allowed to come to this location on RINGS. It was a very exclusive invitation and the meetings here were infrequent. The last meeting was conducted five hundred years ago. Sean and Shay were new at that meeting. They were only observers of the entire process. This time, they each had a question for Gabriel.

Chapter 13

PRE-MEETING

The elite group of Travelers chosen to come to RINGS, considered it an honor. These select Travelers, in any state, whether natural or flight ready, had the awe-inspiring privilege to experience the joy and tranquility of observing wonderous and beautiful sights like none other. They were additionally rewarded with the benefit of unencumbered language from every type, shape, and size of visitor.

Their thoughts were clearly understood, and each had universally positive "internal comments" and observations about what they were seeing and experiencing at C3. C3's internal system of food distribution and delivery was a mystery, but wondrously efficient. Food orders for everyone were intimated directly to the kitchen cooks. Each order was skillfully prepared to the individuals' specifications and delivered via C3 food service staff using Flash speeds. Any passing thoughts of skepticism about receiving cold food, were impressively dashed by the use of Flash speeds allowing the food deliveries to be hot and fresh, as ordered, all the way out on Hexagonal Landing 4.

Time flew by. It was 2:15 p.m. when Shay verbally stated to his group, "We'd better get up to Hexagonal Landing 48 before the Commander gets there."

"Right!" Sean and the others agreed.

Each one intimated, "See you there," to the rest of the group as they disappeared one by one.

Gary Sparkz said, "I'm right behind you guys." He finished his meal and, gone. After teleporting back to the meeting spot early, they noticed that even at this location there was an awesome viewing location of the high and low traveling activities within the sphere. They were all enjoying this level of viewing, unaware of time going by, when…

"Attention! TST's!" Commander Kray had just teleported into their midst. They snapped to attention as he made his way to the front of the group. "At ease, greys." To which they all let their stomachs slouch. "My, my, you greys present quite the sight against this pure crystal background and environment. I wanted to inform those of you who are attending the meeting here on RINGS for the first time, what you should expect and how to act," said the Commander. "Similar to, but even much more so, akin to Zoom Mission Convoy control, the Commander has absolute control of all mission crafts, whether they are Plates or ORBs. Well, here at these conferences, the speaker has, and demands full and complete control over every attendee."

The Commander continued, "The reason should be obvious. One being is intimating to thousands and there is no repeating, unless the speaker is emphasizing a point, by repeating something into your brain. Therefore, the manner and method of conducting the upcoming meeting will be completely at the discretion of the speaker."

"We, as attendees, by default will give the speaker our undivided attention," the Commander emphasized. "The missions that we've all volunteered to complete, plus our Universal Agreement with the mission's objectives are what qualifies us to be here. So, let's all keep our minds open to being receptive to our speaker's teachings. Every soul is encouraged to evaluate for themselves if the speaker remains true to the principles of peace, love, and harmony, and believe me, for twenty millennium before today, hundreds of millions of souls have confirmed what we do is Truth," he explained.

"So, once you're in your seat. You will be connected to the speaker, as if you are in a one-on-one conversation. Yet, you are there and here to listen and receive. Which means, DO NOT LET YOUR MINDS WANDER. I will now say it out loud verbally again. DO NOT LET YOUR MINDS WANDER. Although only the Speaker may be able to hear your thoughts, he obviously doesn't want to hear back from anyone today," the Commander thought, going back to intimating. "Do I make myself clear, gentlegreys?"

The Commander intimated as he glanced across the entire fleet of eyes fixed upon him. "Yes, Sir!" they each thought, as they nodded their heads in confirmation.

"Okay, TST's, let's make our planet proud of us today. Let's teleport to our assigned seats sent from C3's conference director. I'll check in with you all at the end of the day. Fleet dismissed!" the Commander barked, and then disappeared.

Chapter 14

GABRIEL IMPARTS

Gary Sparkz's seat was in amongst all different sizes and types of Travelers. He looked from side to side, up, and around behind him, for just one familiar face, but to no avail. Not one member of his Planet Fleet was in sight. He was seated in what seemed like a stadium. The seats were in mid-air, and they encompassed the entire upper atmosphere of C3's sphere, with C3's 700 story building well below the entire circle of attendees.

Remembering his commander's instructions and observing every soul around him to be stoic and staring straight ahead. He decided to stop being fidgety and assume a calm demeanor for what was about to occur. At 3:00 p.m. from the upper portion of the sphere, it appeared as if the entire group was physically moving up and out of the Sphere.

Gary blinked and confirmed that he was still sitting in mid-air. He was ready for the speaker. But again, from the bottom of his seat, he felt as if they were all now literally, (the way it felt and looked to his eyes), moving up and out of RINGS, heading for who knows where. The atmosphere changed from relative clarity to a soft hue of light, like fog.

Gary could only see about fifteen feet in front of him. Then, a soft clear strong voice began to speak. "Greetings, Gary, I'm very pleased to see you."

"Okay!" Gary thought, "I'm a TST, I've been able to handle everything thrown at me so far. Why does the speaker, whoever

68

he is, know me, out of all these tens of thousands of Travelers?" As Gary was trying to zest these thoughts from his head, remembering the Commander's instructions, an image of what looked like the face of a human appeared directly in front of him. It spoke to him in the same voice he had just heard.

"My name is Gabriel. I know each one of you here individually. I am speaking to each of you now, separately, in person, face to face, so that there is no confusion or misunderstandings. At the end of my discussions with you, I may ask you if you have any questions for me."

"I'm interested in your ability to know and understand truth. Before I begin, I will allow you to take a moment and clear your thoughts. You must be prepared to receive what I will be imparting to you."

From fifteen feet away, Gary noticed the human face begin changing to look more like one of his familiar grey leaders, as he was staring at him. Gary glanced left and right to see if his neighbors were equally entranced, but there were no neighbors. It was as if he alone had been lifted up, out and away from everyone else, where moments ago, thousands had been sitting side by side.

Gary was uncomfortable, avoiding eye contact with the calm and patient gaze looking at him. "How, where, and when, would I have ever known a Human? How is Commander Kray dealing with this face-to-face situation?"

"All right, Gary," he thought to himself. "Get your act together. Stop your thoughts from racing. Just calm down. Look the teacher in the eyes like an experienced TST and learn what he has to teach."

As soon as Gary looked at each of Gabriel's eyes confidently, without making a sound, Gabriel said, "I think you're ready now Gary. Don't worry about being confused, I'll clarify everything I impart to you. Let's begin," Gabriel said.

The introduction between Gabriel and Gary lasted from 3:03 p.m. until 3:08 p.m. Gabriel continued imparting wisdom, understanding, knowledge and truth to everyone between 3:09 p.m. until 5:58 p.m.

"…and that concludes the information I was sent here to impart to you today. How do you feel Gary?" asked Gabriel. Gary felt confident. He exuded the countenance of a changed grey. He blinked his eyes, looked squarely into Gabriel's eyes, and nodded his head several times in humble understanding, acceptance, and agreement about all he had received.

"Thank you," Gary mouthed with his lips in sync with his thought.

"You're all welcome!" Gabriel said, as his image retracted and grew to an immense size in the sky before them.

"All welcome?" wondered Gary, and then he noticed he was back in the midst of tens of thousands of Travelers sitting side by side.

No more fog, just a clear projected image of Gabriel's face up and out before the entire bank of hovering seated guests. To Gary, Gabriel looked just like he could have come from GREY3110227. Gary struggled to see individual Travelers across the expanse to the other side of the massive circular space. He wanted to see if those guests were looking at the back of Gabriel's head or if they were somehow seeing what his side was seeing. It became obvious to Gary that every single individual Traveler had received a perfect vision of Gabriel's teaching and farewell. Each one had an individual interaction and imparting, so of course everyone was somehow looking at his face.

"I look forward to seeing you all again, in five hundred

years!" Gabriel said. "Peace, Love and Harmony to you all. So long!" And with that salutation, Gabriel was gone.

The Travelers found themselves hovering again, back inside the top portion of the C3's sphere with the 700 story Crystal building beautifully shining below them. Gary sat in his plush hovering seat, pondering the marvelous and transformative information that had been presented. He noticed large sections of the sky directly across from him begin to clear up as some of the Travelers, seats, and all were disappearing.

Whole sections of seating on the left and right sides across from him, were beginning to disappear in a rolling fashion. Open space was moving in both directions around the circumference of their massive stadium, as more and more Travelers and stadium were disappearing. Gary was anxiously observing this wave of disappearance coming toward him from both directions when he received an "intimated announcement" from C3's Conference Director.

"Your section is now dismissed! Thanks for coming." Just as Sean, Shay and the others were noticing that Gary (who was previously standing among them before the meeting) was still missing; they felt Gary's static charge, as he materialized right next to Shay. Gary found himself back on Hexagonal Landing 48, standing next to Sean, Shay, and the rest of their previous viewing party from Hexagonal Landing 4.

Apparently, they had all been teleported remotely from the sky arena back to their previous locations by C3's Conference Director. In fact, to the very spots from which they'd previously been standing. It was clear to Gary that there was a lot of information about the powers of teleportation and space-time travel that he didn't understand.

"EXCELLENT!" announced Commander Kray. "We're all

here. I have just a couple of questions for you greys before we break up to prepare for our return home. First, how many of you had questions for Gabriel?" the Commander asked. Eight of the sixty TST's physically raised their hands. As murmurs and inquisitive looks appeared from many of the TST's, Gary remembered that Gabriel didn't ask him if he had any questions, even though he had said he might.

"Okay, last question," stated the Commander. "How many of you are surprised that anyone had a personal question and answer session with Gabriel?" About fifty-two physical hands went up. This number was due to the fifty-two first trip TST's and the seven other senior TST's, along with Commander Kray, who were making this trip for at least their second time. "The math still works!" the Commander exclaimed vocally.

"The miracle that is Gabriel, is beyond any Traveler's understanding. Who or what Gabriel is, is less important than the information he imparts. It's been a long day, so enjoy seeing the sights and then get a good night's sleep. We'll bivouac at 9:00 a.m. tomorrow morning back up at the Arrival and Departure Port Docks. Plan to flush and shower there, then we'll Intimate back to GREY at 10:30 a.m. Any questions? That's all." Receiving no questions, the Commander dismissed the greys.

Chapter 15

THIRTY YEARS LATER

Thirty years passed. Significant things had happened throughout the universe and on planet GREY03110227 since their meeting on RINGS. As it turned out, the most influential grey on planet GREY03110227 became Zing Zong. Yes, Zing and not Zak.

Zing's pathway to becoming such a prominent grey, was highly unlikely. His fortunes dramatically changed in thirty years of time. To understand how this happened, we'll take you back in time after the following summary of events to date.

Commander Kray had retired from Convoy Mission Leadership but remained within DPFA as a liaison to the DPF in various other valuable ways. President Uda Quay remained the active and exuberant President of DPF Administration and Betty remained his long-time administrative assistant. Sean Westix TST, and Shay Kromblay TST, had each received promotions to Zoom Mission Convoy Commands, and had excelled in Convoy Mission leadership on various missions within the Southern, Western, Northern and Eastern Galaxies. Gary Sparkz, TST continued developing and gaining experience on galactic missions.

Zaxson "Zak" Zong TST, had progressed to becoming a Translucent Space/Time Traveler. He currently had 1,150 ORB missions and 866 Teleportation credits officially logged. Zing Zong had been promoted to Vice President of DPFA. He had become President Uda Quay's "go-to grey" for all things administrative and operations related. He also remained active in the engineering and craft development arenas.

It was in his capacity of Test Directing the planets newest Plate crafts, that Zing made history a second time on GREY3110227. As the premiere leader of the DPFA's Engineering wing, Zing became THE first grey to be awarded a gold medal for the largest transport vehicle ever constructed. This planetary recognition and award were the first of its kind ever awarded to a non TST. Their New "V Plates," continued in production and have been successful on thousands of planetary expeditions, to both Planet 5 and Earth combined.

The new Plates were designed to be Fortress Class Star Cruisers, which followed a similar pattern in functionality to that of other Planetary Traveler Crafts. This development was how Zing's fame and recognition was achieved the second time. He received his first award and recognition by becoming the only Gabriel Award winner from Planet GREY3110227. No other GREY inhabitant had ever received such an award. It was bestowed upon Zing (who at that time was just an Engineering Director for DPFA) specifically for becoming the first non-Director or TST to "officially" make personal contact with and communicate/interview another planetary being. These two unprecedented awards, both obtained by Zing, established him as the most heralded citizen ever of Planet GREY3110227.

Now, for the rest of the story, hold on tight. We're going to Flash back in time twenty-seven years ago. Ready? Zoom! Gone.

Chapter 16

27 YEARS AGO

Sixty GREY planet TSTs had returned home from their mission to RINGS. They'd realized the plans they had left on their Mission Planning Boards were now no longer adequate and would need to be significantly broadened. They would increase coordination and collaboration between Travelers from throughout the North, West, and Eastern Quadrants of infinity. The combined efforts of the Travelers were aimed toward gathering and saving as many souls or Heart Propelled intelligent beings as possible.

Based upon the information received from Gabriel, specifically by the eight senior GREY TST's, they knew that time was quickly running out. The number of those to save from destruction were still short of ABOVE's goal. The Inter-Planetary Communication (IPC) discussions had been active and lively, with constant news of happenings throughout infinity. There was even news of rescues and losses from planetary explosions.

Mission Planets continue sending senior Travelers and Convoys on separate and coordinated missions throughout all of infinity, as the work to please ABOVE went forth. In this present day, three years after the RINGS expedition, many Zoom Mission Convoys had been sent to the NORTH Quadrant to aid one of their Mission Planets, BLACK011921. On this planet, they had a volatile and potentially destructive, growth of hatred upon one of their neighboring Planets.

Planet 5 was located eighteen lightyears further to the North of BLACK011921. In another sector of the universe, GREY3110227 had its own neighboring planet that was also a lively topic of IPC news and discussions. Fifty-three lightyears North of GREY3110227, Earth, or the Blue Planet as it was formerly known, was on infinite watch as a constant destination for Travelers throughout infinity. They had varying degrees of success with souls on that Planet. Both Earth and Planet 5 were seen as current critical subjects, susceptible to self-induced cataclysmic destruction.

As of GREY's most recent Zoom Mission Convoys to both Planet 5, and to Earth, many voluntary or requested extractions had been made of Planetary inhabitants. On GREY3110227, some of their new inhabitants had enlightened greys through guest lecturing at DPF Administration Conference Presentation Meetings or assisting missions in other important ways.

This very day, we find Zing sitting in attendance at the DPFA Graduation Ceremony for the latest NSD and TST graduates.

"Congratulations K!" said Zing, at the end of the graduation ceremony. "I'm very proud of you for becoming a TST." Zak had just completed his extensive training and physiological conditioning requirements to become a Translucent Space and Time Traveler. His class had twelve graduates from the sixty-three Directors that were enrolled in the advancement program. The other fifty-one were in various stages of program completion and would have to wait for future months to become eligible to graduate.

"Thanks, G!" Zak said excitedly. Remembering their longstanding discussions about how best to celebrate this achievement, the brothers had to decide where to take Zing for his initial personal ORB flight.

Zak asked, "Have you decided where you want me to Intimate you to?"

"Yeah, I've finally made up my mind," Zing said. "I would like to go to Planet BLACK011921. I've learned that they've been having successful contacts with inhabitants of other planets up there," Zing thought.

"Wow," Zak replied. "That would be a fascinating destination."

"Great!" Zak actually said out loud to his brother. "This will be a great challenge for me and a fabulous experience for you."

"When can we go?" Zing asked.

Contemplating the planning he'd have to do, Zak thought, about three weeks from this day would be a good time frame to plan for their departure. He knew he'd have to fulfill missions already on the books and Zing would have to clear his Engineering schedule as well.

"Let's plan for three weeks from tomorrow, G."

So, the date was set. Zak had a previous connection with one of Planet BLACK's TSTs and decided to contact him on his Commander's IPC Monitor to set up a visit. Zak reached out to Zarkos Bright, TST, a Planet BLACK011921 missionary Traveler. Their planet was in the Kryos Galaxy of the Northern Sector of Infinity. Zarkos was more than willing to accept their visit and booked it into his planning schedule.

The three weeks flew by. Two days before the brothers were to Intimate to Planet BLACK011921, Zak shared with Zing that his last Mission, purely by coincidence, was a joint EAST and SOUTH Sector Zoom Mission Convoy to Planet 5, (which is in BLACK011921's Northern Sector of Infinity). This recent mission went into the very Galaxy and Planet where Zarkos Bright had experienced his successful inhabitant contacts and extractions.

During the mission, Zak had heard from his new Commander Oleanis, that Zarkos had made a significant extraction of Planet 5's Supreme Leader. "Wow," thought Zing. He had no idea this much "contact" activity was happening on 5.

His second choice was going to be visiting Earth, but now he was really glad about his choice of planets to visit. Unknown to Zing, Zak had reached out and firmed up logistical details with Zarkos for their trip. Zak received final approval from Commander Oleanis to sign-out an ORB from the CAD's "Active" Crafts Logbook.

This was going to be an unofficial "Honor trip" to Planet 5, for the two passengers. Zak also instructed Zing on a list of things he must learn and do, in preparation for their trip. The next morning was departure day. Early on flight day, the brothers awoke, ate a light breakfast, just enough to keep their pending flushing to a minimum and walked together the quarter mile to the DPFA compound.

On this morning they would arrive to the DPF together. Zak headed towards the DPFA building to sign out his ORB and FGO. Zing entered the DPF's Departing Missions door to begin his flight preparation. Zak reviewed the authorizations for him and his brother to take this trip, signed them and was issued an FGO for his ORB, both of which he signed out for in the CAD logbook.

Entering the DPF flush area, Zak dropped his FGO into a tray as his attendant escorted him past his brother's cubicle to an adjoining unit. Zing was already rendered unconscious and was in the process of getting flushed, per item three on his list. When

Zak entered the DPF flush area, Zing awoke seven minutes later. Upon exiting his cubicle, he waited for his brother.

"Ready, G?" asked Zak.

"Yep, although I don't know how you guys ever get used to this flushing business," Zing said.

"Ha ha," Zak chuckled to himself.

Zing would be his first guest passenger. He pointed to the Director's tram and intimated for Zing to take that one, he in turn stepped onto the TST Tram. As Zing was moving along and getting sprayed (like he'd never been sprayed before from all angles) he took note of the bright flash of X-ray proofing his brother had just absorbed. As Zing was nearing the end of the tram, he was admiring his fresh-looking svelte shrink-wrapped looking physique, when he again noticed a bright flash that came from within his brother's body.

"Wow, what the flush was that, K?" Zing asked his brother out loud.

"Ah, it's just the reflexive confirmation of our translucence phasing which our bodies react to when triggered," Zak said in reply as they were coming to the end of their Tram ride.

"I knew you were doing lots of training in that TST program, but this physiological transformation stuff is way above my pay grade," Zing said, as he followed his brother out of the DPF.

Recognizing how separated engineering was from chemical science and metabolism genetics, Zak was proud for both he and his brother for their high levels of achievement. On the way out of the DPF the attendants handed Zak his FGO and Zing his note pad and his small carrying bag. Turning right as they exited the DPF they headed toward the ORB docking stations. Zing placed his notepad into his bag and looped it over his shoulder. Everything took on a higher level of anticipation and excitement for Zing. Although he was very familiar with Plates and ORBs from an engineering perspective, he had only seen and worked on the crafts at their engineering wing of the facilities. He had not been on the active dock pads prior to a live mission.

The engineering wing of DPF had their own separate departure pad for test flights of developing crafts. Zak turned left past the fifteenth ORB hovering in line. He was exchanging pleasantries and acknowledging several other TSTs that were coming and going around the crafts. Down the aisle past another five rows of ORBs, they arrived at their craft.

Stepping up and into the next one on his right, Zak called to his brother, "Welcome aboard, G!" Zing followed but halted just outside the doorway, taking in the magnificence of this beautiful sleek metallic ORB.

"Come on aboard," his brother Intimated.

Cautiously, Zing stepped into the round cylindrical metal sphere. There was very little to observe. To his left he could see what looked like the outline of a doorway without any handle or window. To his right there was what looked like a partition for separating the craft from where he and his brother were now standing.

"Okay," said his brother, I'm gonna prepare you for our trip" Zak intimated. "Did you read your "Passenger Transit Manual (PTM)?" Zak asked verbally.

"Yep," replied Zing. "It was on the list."

"Great," thought Zak, knowing how thorough his engineering brother would be. "Stand there within that square area for me, G. I'll see you there," said Zak, as he placed his FGO into its holder on the far wall of the ORB and pressed several buttons on a panel next to it.

"Okay," replied Zing as he stood still, with his arms folded across his chest. As Zak leaned back against the back wall of the ORB, an announcement was audibly heard within the craft. "SECURING OBD FOR TRANSITION," broadcasted audibly within the ORB.

A white mist began to envelope Zing. It lifted him and sealed him with a porous yet secure antigravity blanket of protection, like a white bubble wrap within the sphere. He was no longer in contact with the floor, walls, or ceiling of the craft. Zak had leaned back against the wall of the ORB, into what looked like the slight outline of an upright cushion, into which he then disappeared. "DESTINATION CONFIRMED," broadcasted audibly within the ORB.

There was silence within the ORB, and silence outside the ORB as it slowly rose to sixty feet above the ORB departure pad. A brilliant flash of light. Gone.

Chapter 17

ZARKOS BRIGHT

Planet BLACK011921, was so far north in the Universal Cosmos that its nearest sun star was located below the planet's southern pole. This meant that their planet rotated in almost complete darkness perpetually. The only light was the light from distant galaxies and stars, giving off dim illumination twenty-four hours daily. The instantly luminous flash of light signaling the arrival of Zak's ORB, rippled across the surface of the planet like a firecracker.

Zarkos had prepared the reception party by instructing all guests to shield their eyes from the Arrival Dock Pad, which had been prepared for Zak's arrival. Zak materialized within his ORB, pressed and de-pressed various portions of his wall control panel to re-materialize the ORB. He docked the ORB upon the planet's cushion of magnetism. Lastly, he retracted the safety shielding encompassing Zing.

Grabbing his FGO from its holder, "Let's meet our host, G," Zak instructed, as Zing's feet were just reaching the floor of the craft.

"You okay?" asked Zak.

There was no way Zing was going to tell his brother that he felt miserable. In fact, if he had not been flushed before this trip, anything within his body at that moment, would have been involuntarily expelled from him through any orifice available.

"Just a little woozy" replied Zing, wobbling, and following

his brother out of the ORB. As Zak reached out both hands to embrace Zarkos' extended hands, Zing recognized how different BLACKs were from greys.

Although he was still very lightheaded, he felt his senses slowly coming back to him. They were all bigger, stronger looking, and their eyes glowed in a yellow hue.

"Zarkos, this is my brother Zing," Zak said, turning to introduce his brother. Two large hands reached down to Zing, to which Zing lifted his own hands up to have them engulfed into each of Zarkos' big hands.

"Welcome to BLACK011921 Zing," he heard Zarkos tell his mind. "We're very pleased to have you here as our guests."

"A pleasure," Zing intimated. "Please, accept these gifts."

Zarkos instructed an aide to hand goggles and vests to each guest. The goggles will assist your vision and the vests will assist your ability to keep up with movements here as well."

"Yikes," Zing thought to himself, more movement. Fortunately, his thoughts chimed in amongst other well-wishes sent their way from their hosts.

"I am here to answer any questions you have during your stay here with us. Shall we go?" asked Zarkos.

The reception party turned and walked toward what looked like a multi-decked rectangular box, Zing looked up and behind him as he was following and simultaneously donning his vest. He saw huge crafts in stationary positions in multiple vertical rows high above their dock location. "How do they get in and out of those vehicles?" he thought, as he entered the box and was directed to a second tier seat above and next to where Zarkos and Zak were seated.

"Typically, we teleport everywhere on our Planet, Zing" Zarkos offered in response to Zings thoughts. "We only have this singular deck pad for the various visitors to our planet."

"Thanks," Zing replied in thought.

With a slight jolt, the box took off. Everything appeared so dark to Zing. He was pleased to feel that the vest was holding everything in place and giving him a slight sense of comfort. He remembered he was holding a pair of goggles. He slipped them on. Everything was really different with these things on. The box was a smooth surfaced conveyance, speeding along as if pulled by an unseen cable or a strong magnet.

The BLACKs were actually dark brown in color, and now, their eyes didn't seem to be glowing. Before Zing could make sense of what he was seeing, he glanced down and to his left, and saw Zak in his natural state, as a grey, purple with yellow dots. He was talking with Zarkos who now looked like a brown skinned thin creature with rounded facial features. The goggles showed the "Natural State" of things, and of themselves, even though they hadn't yet showered off their flight coatings.

"How is this possible?" Zing thought to himself. Outside the windows, the scenery was very appealing. but Zing couldn't tell if he was looking through the glass or if the glass reflected a screen view of a video. Suddenly, they went down into a tunnel which opened to a brightly lit underground city. Zing was taking in the sights of this underground world. Beyond the lights of the city was a stark image illuminating across the horizon. A large cross had been built high up on a hillside.

They arrived at the conference center and were transported into the building via tram. Once inside, they headed to a large meeting room on the left side of the building. "Please, come in and be seated greys," Zarkos intimated. "My time is yours," he said.

Chapter 18

ZINGS EDUCATION

Before he began speaking, Zak asked Zarkos if he would allow him to record their Q and A session. "Of course," Zarkos responded with a wave of his hand. Zak took his FGO out of his vest pocket. He pressed the "Obs" button to begin recording their meeting.

Zarkos proceeded to answer the myriad of questions Zing had about life on BLACK011921, their foods, their modes of travel, their familial structures, their types of crafts and of course their missions.

Zarkos shared, that through wisdom, understanding, knowledge and truth, their missions, as with all other planetary missions had been guided from ABOVE. He explained that the successes they'd enjoyed as planetary explorers had been bittersweet. Yes, they had communicated directly with planetary beings, but the outcomes had not been as rewarding as outside perception would indicate.

Zarkos went on to describe the circumstances and timelines of their most recent encounters. With the help of the leadership on Planet EAST446876, many of the occupants throughout their planet decided to convert from hateful thoughts and actions toward becoming believers in the principles of Peace, Love and Harmony.

"We were successful in transporting thousands of these intelligent beings to other planets throughout the galaxies. Yet, we could not alter the destructive events that they had already put into motion. Planet EAST446876, ignited into an exploding star, creating the third Black Hole, residing in Sector: EAST of our infinite universe."

"What about Planet 5?" Zing asked.

"I participated in the communication and extraction of Planet 5's Supreme Leader," replied Zarkos. "In fact, he will be our surprise guest and will be arriving here shortly." With this information Zing froze into a silent stupor. Zarkos went on. "At this very moment, he is being transported here to meet with you both."

Amazed, Zing thought to himself, "Wow, that's more than I could have ever dreamed. How could that happen?"

Hearing Zing's original thought, but not really understanding his true question, Zarkos went on. "We had just found the right light spectrum and frequency to recognize their "Doors" to the entrances of their planet's underground cities. The dimensions that they exist in below surface are the 5th and 6th dimensions."

As Zarkos was sharing the events of finding and rescuing their guest speaker, Zing continued to reflect on his own question. "How could this happen? The Planet 5 Leader is here, on this planet, willing to speak to us; just a couple of nosey guests?" Ultimately, he decided to zest his thoughts, shut up and keep listening.

"It required triangulating of our light spectrum frequencies to visualize their existence," said Zarkos.

"Once found," Zarkos continued, "they saw our crafts and surprisingly, they didn't appear to be afraid. The inhabitants of the sector we flew through were willing to answer our questions. They in turn, shared the location of their leader. As mission leader from our planet, it fell to me to make the contact," said Zarkos.

"I beamed the volunteer creature aboard, and his thoughts steered our Wedge crafts to their Supreme Leader. The notoriety that I've received throughout the galaxy for this find, is far too generously attributed to me. Our entire mission fleet was instrumental in carrying Gabriel's message to these beings. They in turn, have willingly turned away from their former destructive and hateful ways towards each other."

Zarkos continued, "As you will hear from Supreme Leader Kleezard, we may have found them too late to save them, even though there may be a way to save their planet. Whenever we appeared above their midst, we observed their creatures reaching up to our Wedges, not pointing, but reaching up, as if requesting our help."

As Zarkos was sharing his information about Planet 5, technicians entered their meeting room and began setting up lighting standards, mirrors, and a large chair across from them. The lights and mirrors were all pointing toward the empty seat. Some of the light standards did not appear to be ON, yet Zing knew that this merely indicated that those lights were reflecting a different light frequency. Before the technicians left, they set up a large rectangular screen upon the table between the empty chair on one side of the screen and themselves on the other side.

"Apparently, our special guest has just now arrived," announced Zarkos, as he rose to his feet and turned toward the door. Both Zak and Zing also rose and faced the doorway. Zak glanced down to his FGO as he stood to his feet, he wanted to make sure it was still recording, which it was. They heard sliding and shuffling outside the doorway, then a large BLACK attendant followed by another, with a gap between them, seemed to be escorting something or someone into the room that was completely invisible to Zak and Zing.

"I can't see anything," Zing whispered to Zak.

The two BLACK planet attendants walked slowly, as if holding onto invisible arms, Zarkos stated, "You're not alone. I can't see him either in our dimension's lighting."

As one of the attendants pulled the invisible creatures chair back to make room for the Supreme Leader, they could see flashing across the screen and across one of the mirrors. In front of them of a bluish colored creature with a wide body and a thick tail tucked along his side as he sat down before them. "Forgive my need for assistance, the gravitational forces of this Planet are much greater than what we're accustomed," Supreme Leader Kleezard intimated to the three hosts.

The Supreme Leader curiously moved his head in a rotating manner, as if casting his thoughts toward them, when he intimated to them.

"Welcome Supreme Leader Kleezard" announced Zarkos, as he, Zak, and Zing returned to their seats. "Our guests here with us today are Zak and Zing Zong, from Planet GREY3110227, of the SOUTH Sector of our infinite universe."

"Greetings to you! It's a pleasure to meet and visit with you all," intimated the Supreme Leader, as he shook his head in their direction. "You can call me Ploy, a name I'm called by my friends. We can be informal here," the Supreme Leader said.

Chapter 19

WHY 5 IS DYING

"Thank you, Ploy," intimated Zarkos, "for being willing to meet and to visit with us here today. I'm equally thankful to our guests who have come from such a long distance to join us" he continued. "They had no idea that you'd be available to meet with them and be willing to communicate and to share your thoughts. So, although it's quite a surprise, we're honored with your presence."

Ploy responded, "As you well know Zarkos, having saved my life, my family's life, and the lives of countless others from my planet, it is I who have the privilege of meeting and spending time with each of you. How may I serve you today?" Ploy asked. Both Zarkos and Zak simultaneously looked at Zing, who was still entranced at the mere presence of Ploy.

To Zing, Ploy's head resembled a large fish with dull horns. His body appeared to be of a large lizard like creature, with differing shades of green splotches all over and a thick tail. His large legs and three toed feet definitely did not indicate speed, no matter what planet he might be on.

The three guest hosts were observing Ploy through both the screen before them and the Orb in front of them, which displayed Ploy's entire body image. Zing startled out of his trance and noticed that Ploy, Zarkos, and Zak were all looking at him.

"Oh! Ah! Yes, I have just a few questions for you, Ploy, if you'd be so kind as to answer, that would be great," Zing requested.

"Absolutely!" Ploy responded with a shake of his head.

"What Dimension controls your planet 5?" Zing asked.

"We live and occupy the fifth and sixth dimensional space times on our planet. This evolutionary micro-dimensional plurality enables us to utilize space/time to our advantage in cramped settings as our underground dwelling spaces dictate," said Ploy.

"What crafts do you use on your planet for extra Planetary travels?" Zing intimated.

"We are not interstellar travelers," replied Ploy. "However, we can and do teleport, but we are restricted to the two dimensions upon our planet's surface. It is cumbersome for us to travel into two-dimensional space. We had not developed the ability nor the inquisitiveness to leave our planet; that is until recently."

"What's changed, Ploy?" intimated Zing.

Shaking his head, a little violently, Ploy began intimating by looking up at the ceiling and rocking his head back and forth. "There are other 5's on our planet that do not wish for peace, love and harmony! They wish for evil destruction of other 5's that look like me and my kind." Ploy continued. "They look exactly as we do on my planet, except they are absent any pigment in their outer skin layers. They appear as pale colored 5's and they desire to either eliminate or restrict to Dimension 5, all non-pale 5's," said Ploy still shaking his head. "They have crafted special destructive metals and have created chemical accelerants which have been tested and proven to be devastating weapons of death."

"Yes," Zarkos interjected, "it was the intergalactic disturbance within interstellar space that first drew our attention to Planet 5. Over these past few decades, we've been convinced that the "Pale 5's" have absolutely no willingness to turn away from their destructive ends."

"We don't know how much more time we have as 5's to remain as life forms within the Cosmos," intimated Ploy, "but us green 5's are ready to re-patriate as effectively as we can before Planet 5 becomes the next star to self-ignite within our solar system."

"Believe me," offered Zarkos, "your planet is way too close to having a Black Hole show up and to be formed in our region of space." Zing's head was spinning. He was asking questions and getting answers, but the pain he observed in Ploy while he was describing the plight being experienced on his planet was like nothing he'd ever heard before.

Planet GREY3110227 was populated by benevolent souls desiring the best for everyone on it. In fact, the DPF Administration's goal was spreading peace, love, and harmony to planet's wherever they may be. Planet BLACK011921's mission was trying to accomplish the same goal when they discovered Planet 5.

Returning his gaze and eye contact to Zing, Ploy intimated, "Were it not for the efforts of planets like BLACK and GREY and others, the Cosmos would be full of exploding stars. I believe some of these explosions were caused through self-inflicted detonations by selfish, oblivious, occupants who decided if they couldn't have their own way within their planet, then it was better to just blow it and themselves up into eternity. So, thank you again, Zarkos."

"No, thank you, Ploy," responded Zing, looking back to Zarkos, with a look of "that's all I have."

"Zak, do you have any questions for Ploy?" asked Zarkos.

"No," said Zak. "I don't have any questions for Ploy, but I

did just want to say this. I have been sitting here absolutely amazed at the questions and responses about something that both myself and Zarkos are intimately aware of as we conduct our missions."

"Having been on hundreds of missions," said Zak, "a fraction of those Zarkos has conducted I'm sure, yet I'm humbled to hear about the pain and suffering that persists within our Cosmos. Zarkos mentioned about the explosions observed and felt up here within your Northern Sector, perpetrated by Planet 5 and the risk to interstellar spatial continuity that exists with their localized threat. We, likewise, have a potential for explosion on a planet called Earth within our Southern Sector of the Cosmos. It seems they are equally bent on self-destruction. There is hatred among and against other life forms upon that planet and a willingness to blow their entire world up if they cannot have unilateral superiority over all other inhabitants of their World. We are late to the game of intervention, and this will be our focus moving forward, I promise. That's all I have."

"Friends," said Ploy, "I have enjoyed our visit. It was good for me to release some pent-up emotions that I've been carrying for a long time now. Forgive me if I've offended you in any way, but I am so grateful to have been saved from my planet and continue to hope for better things and times moving forward. Realistically, I am not expecting any change whatsoever. Thank you, thank you kindly," Ploy intimated.

Zarkos had previously pressed the attendant button and at Ploy's concluding remarks, the two big BLACK planet attendants returned to retrieve Ploy.

As they walked over toward him, Zarkos, Zing, and Zak stood respectfully. "Our many, many thanks to you Supreme Leader Kleezard," Zarkos intimated as Ploy was being helped to his feet and exiting his spot from across the table. His thick green tail was the last image of Ploy that any of them saw as he was assisted out through the doors toward an awaiting transporter.

Zak reached out, grabbed his Orb, and clicked OFF his Obs button. "Do you have time for a meal?" asked Zarkos. Zing was starving.

"I would love to say yes," replied Zak, "but our planet has peculiar flight rules." Placing his FGO back inside the pocket of his vest, Zak informed Zarkos and his brother that while on missions of any kind, Directors and TSTs were not allowed to consume any foods. They were only allowed to consume liquids, which were present onboard their crafts. These were sufficient and not detrimental to their physiologies during teleportation's.

"I understand," countered Zarkos. "I presume you'll want to be transported back to your craft then?"

"Yes please, if that can be arranged," replied Zak.

"Absolutely!" said Zarkos. As they walked toward the conference center exits, they exchanged pleasantries of mutual amazement of the meeting they had just left.

Outside now, standing before the transport vehicle, which Zarkos had intimated for their return transportation, Zarkos faced them and said, "I will say my goodbyes here then," as he extended his hands to both Zak and then to Zing. "Peace, Love and Harmony to you both. I look forward to future meetings with you both. This has been a very nice and informative visit, and I thank you both for coming to make it possible," Zarkos concluded.

"The same to you," they both intimated simultaneously.

The brothers turned and entered the transporter and were shortly back at their ORB. Zing assumed his previous position. Zak replaced his FGO back into its holder which brought the

ORB to life as it sealed the exterior door and began spraying the on-board deck to prepare Zing for transit. Zak leaned into his far wall cushion and disappeared. "SECURING OBD FOR TRANSITION" audibly sounded within the ORB. "DESTINATION CONFIRMED" audibly sounded within the ORB next.

There was silence within the ORB, and silence outside the ORB as it slowly rose to twenty feet. The ORB sequenced the appropriate distance from and between the other BLACK planet Wedge Crafts (which were scattered in a hovering layer all over and around their Departure Dock location). A brilliant flash of light. Gone.

Chapter 20

UNFORTUNATE PRIVILEGE

Within four hundred milliseconds, or the blink of an eye, there was a brilliant flash of light, signaling the appearance of Zak and Zing's ORB, stationary at sixty feet above GREY3110227's departure dock. From there, their metallic sphere began slowly descending to its three-foot resting hover above the docks pad.

Once again, Zing felt extremely queasy. But like before, he didn't want his brother to know. He struggled to manage the nausea. Zing was really glad he hadn't eaten anything on BLACK011921. Zing's mind was racing as the ORB craft unwrapped him from his thermodynamically sealed covering, allowing his wobbly feet to settle onto the on-board deck (OBD) surface. As he stepped or stumbled forward from the OBD, he nudged his brother who was standing near the departure door, light years away in deep thought.

"You okay, K?" Zing asked his brother.

Startled, Zak said," Oh yeah, Wow, what a meeting, and an experience right?"

"Yeah," Zing replied, following his brother out of the ORB. "I was hoping to get an opportunity to hear some war stories from other TST's with field experience. It was more than I ever wished for, to be able to actually communicate with another sentient being."

As they walked up the pad and turned right onto the dock toward the DPF, Zak said, "I think you need to come with me G."

"Why?" asked Zing looking at his brother as they walked toward the DPF Administration Building.

"Well, I have to log my FGO back in at the CAD, but before I do, I'm pretty sure I need to run this thing by Commander Oleanis."

"Why do you have to do that?" asked Zing.

"Well…" they were just about to reach the door and before Zak could respond, the door to the DPF Administration building opened in front of them and one of the CAD Clerks began to clap as he was ushering the brothers into the building.

"What's this about" Zing asked as he followed his brother through the doorway and down the hallway leading to the Commander's office.

"I knew it," thought Zak.

"Knew what?" said Zing aloud! Both sides of the hallway were lined with Clerks, administrators, and other personnel from within the DPF and all of them were clapping their hands. Further down the hallway near the Commander's office, standing outside and clapping were a few Directors and TST's, shouting congratulations to Zing.

Zak turned and entered the Commander's office, Zing followed and asked aloud, "Why are they all clapping for me, K?"

Entering the Commander's office, Zing saw Commander Oleanis standing behind his desk and pointing to the seat in front of his desk. "Sit down here, Engineer," the Commander urged to Zing. Looking at his brother, who nodded his head toward the chair that the Commander was pointing to, Zing complied, sat down, and turned his gaze back to the Commander.

"Well, Zing Zong, you're responsible for breaking your brother's Obs Channel!"

"What?" thought Zing. "How on GREY did I do that?" he thought again, bewildered.

"President Quay is on his way here now because you've done something that no other grey has ever done before today. You've communicated to and interviewed another Planetary being," responded Commander Oleanis.

"But isn't that what happens, on every mission sent out from here?" Zing thought.

"Yes, you're right Zing, but we send out highly trained and skilled Directors and TSTs, not engineers!" the Commander clarified. "After speaking with Zarkos, on IPC he was equally amazed!" "He just assumed that both you and your brother were TSTs. He had no idea that an untrained Space-Time Traveler could survive exposures and the stresses of teleportation over such extreme distances. After your meeting with the President, we'll need to get you over to sick bay and have you checked out for exposure and possible internal issues"

"Great," thought Zing. Just getting out of his "Spanx like" travel coating would do wonders for him.

"MAKE WAY FOR THE PRESIDENT!" An announcement came from the hallway. Into the Commander's office came two Aides, followed by President Uda Quay. Walking right over to Zing, who was just standing up and turning around, the President grabbed and hugged him.

"Zing Zong, you are now and forever more, our planet's first, non-trained, grey to communicate with another planet's creatures. This news has reached ABOVE, and I have already heard from Gabriel, who has authorized our planet's first ever Gabriel Award. It will be awarded to you in a celebration at our next scheduled Zoom Mission Convoy Presentation Meeting. I just wanted to express my personal, sincere appreciation to both you, and your brother Zak, for so positively representing our planet to ABOVE as an example of new ways to extend peace, love, and harmony throughout the Cosmos. Now, anything you need, just ask Betty, and I'll see that it gets done for you. And that goes for you too, Zak," the President said as he turned and exited the Commanders office.

"MAKE WAY FOR THE PRESIDENT!" An announcement went forward down the hallway ahead of the President as he exited the Commander's office. "Okay, you greys, clear out of here, I've got work to do. Zak, don't forget to sign your FGO back in, and get your brother showered and fed. I have you scheduled to report back for duty in two days," the Commander barked.

"Yes, Sir, Commander, Sir," Zak replied as he followed his brother out of the door.

Dropping his Orb off at the desk and signing where the CAD attendant was pointing, Zak caught up with his brother exiting the Administration building. All the way to the showers there were way too many questions flashing through Zings head for Zak to even attempt a response, so he just waited until they entered the locker room before he said, "Listen, G, you're a brilliant Engineer, and you've just had a once in a lifetime experience, accidental though it may be, a life changing experience, nonetheless. So, enjoy what comes next. I'm pleased and happy for you, and I'm glad you're my brother."

Before they had a chance to shower, a Nurse came by and asked Zing to follow him to the examination room. "Hop up on this table for me," the Nurse instructed. Zing hopped up on the table and received a thorough head, eyes, nose, throat, and body exam. "You've been exposed to very high levels of radiation," the Nurse said. "You must have had a heck of a bout with dizziness I'll bet."

"You said it, Doc," Zing replied. "I'm feeling better now though."

"Good," the Nurse said, as he was giving Zing a shot. "You'll be fine in a couple days or so from this."

"What was that?" Zing asked rubbing his shoulder.

"Just Potassium Iodide along with some longer named concoctions that will quickly get you back to yourself in no time."

"Thanks Doc," Zing said.

"You're welcome," the Nurse said. "Now go ahead and get showered, you're clear here."

Zing entered the showers just as Zak was exiting. Zak asked him, "You gonna live, G?"

Washing up as he replied, "Well, at least until I die," Zing thought.

"Not funny!" his brother said aloud. "That was a very dangerous thing we did, G. It's all my fault. It never occurred to me that you might be in danger taking a long trip like that with me."

"Not a problem, K." Zing said, "It gave me design ideas and challenges to think about for our next generation of Crafts."

"I'm glad it all worked out for the best," said Zak.

Zing agreed, "Yep, it was pretty naïve for us to feel just because we could, we should, take any craft and Zoom or teleport wherever we wanted. Obviously, this type of case has never even been anticipated before now," Zak said.

"That's possibly just an unfortunate privilege we have as honored citizens of our planet" Zing replied. "Let's get our furry bodies dried off and go get something to eat."

Chapter 21

V's TO EARTH

Within the next twenty-seven years after arriving back from BLACK011921... Zing had led his engineering group in the development of the New Star Cruiser Class sized V shaped Transporters. Simply called V's. These crafts were capable of Zoom speeds and were also Teleportation Crafts. They were used to advance interstellar planet hopping, while also transporting as many as five hundred grey dignitaries and other select passengers on planetary missions.

Given the immense size of these V's, it was a gigantic engineering feat that these vehicles could also teleport. The creation of this Fortress Class of Star Cruisers is what earned Zing his Gold Medal from President Quay and the honor and praise of every citizen of GREY3110227. Zak Zong, TST (through the work of himself and his crews of Directors) assisted the engineering wing by directing V transporters in test flights and on missions. This work earned Zak the promotional designation and rank of Lieutenant Commander in charge of V Class Star Cruisers.

Five years after the BLACK011921 trip, an IPC News Flash rippled throughout interstellar space. It was an announcement that had to do with a recent Northern Sector Planetary explosion. "IPC NEWS FLASH! The brilliant flash of Starlight observed throughout the Northern Sector of the Cosmos last night was the cataclysmic explosion of Planet 5. After many missionary and evacuation missions to this planet from multiple planets like BLACK011921, GREY3110227, and others, the ultimate tragedy could not be avoided. Efforts extended toward saving all 5's, succumbed to the malicious acts by the hateful few pale 5's. They detonated fifteen strategically placed mega-nuclear bombs, which mushroomed and rippled through openly drilled fissures, igniting the planets core, exploding, and destroying the planet's mantle crust, resulting in the brilliant explosion witnessed remotely across the cosmos."

"Great sadness is reported throughout the Universe for the loss of Planet 5 and all of its heart propelled inhabitants. These hundreds of millions of innocent souls were lost due to the venomous actions of a relative few hateful beings. It must never be forgotten. Planet 5 is no more. The remnants of exploded matter continue to implode downward into the Black Hole created by the absence of weighted mass that previously occupied its universal space. The pale 5's hatred was too great for any planet to sustain."

Present day…

The North, East, South and West Sectors of Interstellar space continue sending missionary crafts to planets like 5, Earth, EAST446876 and others. The missions remain the same, to help where help is needed and requested. The signs and signals sent from the Blue Planet Earth have created a new and unique threat to galactic harmony within the universal cosmos. Its human inhabitants desire to spread their presence and bad intentions to other planets. Earth's past planetary explosions, fires, clear cuttings, massive core extractions, growing pollutions of sky, soils, and oceans have been escalating. Cracks in the Earth's

101

mantle are weakening its ability to hold in its molten core.

Quakes above and below ground, across its planet's surface, even upon its ocean floors are destabilizing planetary structural continuity. Stresses upon this planet are adding to larger and more frequent cyclones, tornados, evaporating lakes, streams, underground wells, and reservoirs. Melting of its massive ice sheets from its North and South polar regions, as well as its mountainous regions show clear indications of planetary destruction and a death march toward extinction. All sectors of universal space have seen from afar and up close, how destructive, and threatening humans are to the entire solar system, if these earthlings are allowed to export their destructive intentions to neighboring planets. Earth itself, as a universal celestial body by any objective observation, is pleading for help. The planet appears infested by a carbon-based life form which is intentionally bent upon killing it. However, Earth may be capable of ridding itself of its disease. Signs from space indicate that the protective ozone shield surrounding the planet may soon be disintegrated, and thus the human infestation will be eliminated.

If this ozone depletion continues, as fully intended by its humans, the open non-oxygenated vacuum of space will complete the undermining of the layers coating the planet's atmosphere. Once penetrated by open space, Earth will begin to cure itself, by eliminating all oxygen and its atmosphere leaving it devoid of all living creatures. This will kill off the human infestation, as well as all other carbon-based life forms. Next will be the depletion of its oceans and remaining waters which also contain oxygen. This will save the planet but eliminate one hundred percent of the inhabitants and living creatures upon it.

Earth has an even larger number of hateful humans, by percentage, than any other planet that has been visited by

Travelers. It is unknown at this time if Earth is salvageable. All sectors of infinity are now on alert to the risks that Earth presents to universal peace, love, and harmony. Previous communications from Travelers for centuries have failed to find a planetary leader.

Using stone constructions, mappings, diagrams and hieroglyphs, images drawn upon crops, land surfaces, and even direct teachings to early humans thousands of years ago did not work. All efforts to teach mission principles, have yielded no change in the direction of this planets path toward self-destruction. Hatred cannot co-exist with peace, love, and harmony. These missions, to preserve and save as many heart-propelled beings as possible, who agree to accept peace, love, and harmony with their fellow inhabitants, will continue as needed throughout infinity.

Until that day when senior missionary Travelers receive a YES answer from the bi-millennium speaker to the following question…

Is there a date and time set?

THE END

GLOSSARY

ABOVE[1] (Upper case) — The unreachable place. Located beyond time and space. Where direction for wisdom, understanding, knowledge and truth is imparted. Each Bi-Millennium, Missionaries[16] or Travelers[28] receive instruction from teachers sent from here. These teachings are spread throughout the infinite cosmos, in search of heart propelled beings and creatures, who desire Peace, Love and Harmony with all other fellow occupants upon their planets.

CAD[2] — Craft Assignment Desk. This is where Directors[6] and TSTs[29] sign-in and sign-out for the Plates[23] or ORBs[21] they will be Directing[6]. Along with acquiring a Craft, they also sign-in and sign-out Flight Guide Orbs (Orbs)[11]. These are effective keys to their Crafts. (But Orbs are much more than keys.) All FGOs (Orbs) are to be returned after every flight. Flight data will be downloaded, reviewed for pertinent Channel[3] activity, scrubbed, and prepared for the next assignments.

Channels[3] — The output from FGO(Orb) broadcasts. These channels are viewed on planet GREY3110227, by its citizens for entertainment and education. All historical and "Live" feeds are cherished as daily education. Each Director and TST is assigned a "Discovery Channel" and their mission observations are the subject matter for their "15 minutes of fame".

Convoys[4] — These are groups of crafts directed under leadership by a Fleet Commander.

Departure Prep Facility (DPF)[5] — This is the large Administration building designated to prepare all Directors for inter-planetary Zoom Missions. NSDs[18] and TSTs[29] must have their bodily systems flushed and thoroughly sprayed with an atmospheric coating which preserves their bodies against all elements and forces of Galactic space travel. The ending process converts pilots[22] from their normal fuzzy purple and yellow color to thin smooth grey pilots or Directors.

Directors[6] — The Rank achieved by ORB and Plate pilots. NSD pilots are Neurologically Connected[17] to the Plates they fly or Direct. TSTs become chemically and anatomically bonded to their ORB crafts through their higher level of Intimation[13] capabilities.

DPF[5] — **Departure Preparation Facility.** This is where Directors and TSTs are prepared for every flight or mission. The DPF is staffed to support zoom missions.

DPFA[7] — **Departure Preparation Facility Administration**. The Administrative overseers of the DPF and the Engineering wings of Planetary Mission Control. It is headed by President, Uda Quay.

EMP[8] — See Electro-Magnetic Pulse[9].

Electro-Magnetic Pulse[9] (EMP) — All Plates and ORBs can detect electronic and digital signals which are connected to threat components of any type of vehicle or target. When initiated, it's called Jam[15] or Jamming. EMP's, when triggered, can thwart any microscopic signals or digital routings toward initiating threat vehicle ignitions. Plate and ORB defenses can intercept and disrupt enemy targeting signals at source for multiple locations along their intended communications track, to effectively eliminate any threat.

(Option 1- At source, or threat vehicle; Option 2- Re-routing of locked-on target references.)

Flash Speed[10] — Sub-Zoom Authorized Speed level. The highest Authorized speed to be traveled inside of any Planet's atmosphere by Plates. (ORBs phase in and phase out at will)

Flight Guide Orb (FGO)[11] — A circular ball, which is more crystal ball than computer, but is yet even more. It controls Plates and ORBs. It can visually display whatever its holder is thinking about. If thought is of a far-off place, the FGO(Orb) will show the location of thought in real-time details. When pre-programmed by Zoom Mission Control[34] Commanders, it visually shows all aspects of planned Zoom missions in 3D. Lastly, it also records audio and visual observations called "Obs", or observations which recordings are beamed instantly through space and time back to DPF Administration.

greys (Lower case)[12] — Although planet inhabitants are known as greys, they are not gray in color. They are purple with splotches of yellow.

The color of all NSD and ORB pilots is however gray in color. This is due to their body transition for flight via the DPF. However, all pilots and other inhabitants of Planet GREY3110227, are as stated, purple with yellow spots: Short in stature, about the size of a typical small child. They are furry or fluffy with three fingers, and three toes. This is their natural state. They are adorable looking and very huggable.

Intimation[13] — An "**official flight command or instruction**". NSDs and TSTs can fly their crafts with their unspoken thoughts. Likewise, when a member of a Convoy Mission, the Convoy Commander controls both flight controls and communications for the entire convoy fleet.

Intimation is what Directs Plates and ORBs to maneuver as instructed by thoughts or telepathy[25].

IPC[14] — **Interstellar-Planetary Communications**. The means of coordinated communications with Super Intelligent Space/Time Travelers, throughout infinity.

Jam[15] — Or Jamming. See Electro-Magnetic Pulse[8].

Missionaries[16] — The description given to Interstellar Space and Time Travelers, beings who are directed by ABOVE[1]. On a Bi-millennium basis, Travelers/Missionaries receive wisdom, understanding, knowledge and truth at prescribed meeting locations. These informed Travelers are then invited by ABOVE to learn, the evolving methods of teaching Peace, Love and Harmony to universal seekers.

Neuro-Connectivity[17] — The condition of neurologically connecting NSD Plate craft pilots physically to their Plate crafts. It involves neurologically grafting the body of the pilots to their crafts through a series of tentacles physically completing the connections. Once melded to become one singular unit, the Director then becomes "THE craft". Flying it is accomplished merely by thinking or "Intimating" flight maneuvers. TSTs have evolved beyond this process. Once cleared by DPFA, TSTs merely step into their sealed Plates or Orbs and are chemically meshed with their crafts.

NSD[18] — Non-Shape Shifting Plate Director. The official designation given to Plate pilots.

OBD[19] — On-Board Deck, typically of an ORB. This is the location to which Visual Beams[30] capture/transport creatures and items onboard and within ORBs.

Opaque Mode[20] — Is the term for changing the inside "Internal viewing" within Plate craft to a synthesized "External viewing" throughout the craft. Another term for looking through the Plate, is called viewing through Visual Panels[31]. Which means that by Toggle switch, allows 360-degree external viewing, while remaining in any externally visible state set by the Plate's Directors or Commanders.

Orb[11] — See Flight Guide Orb (FGO)[11].

ORBs[21] (Upper case) — Another type of GREY Planetary craft. These vehicles can shape shift. Which means the ORB can change its physical properties to become any size, shape, color, metallic or brilliant light. They are exclusively Directed or flown by TST's.

Pilots[22] — There's no term for the word pilots on planet GREY3110227. It's merely used occasionally within this book for association and reference purposes to keep from losing our readers. There are only NSDs and TSTs to fly crafts on this Planet. (Plates, ORBs, & Vs)

Plates[23] — The official designation of the flying crafts which are flown or directed by NSDs. (Plates, ORBs, and Vs are otherwise known as UFOs)

Seekers[24] — Any heart propelled being or creature desiring Peace, Love and Harmony with its other planetary beings and creatures.

Telepathy[25] — Communication of thoughts or commands by means other than speaking.

Teleport[26] — See Teleportation.[27]

Teleportation[27] — The instantaneous method of object movements through Space and Time via telepathy.

Travelers[28] — The pseudo-name given to TSTs who have become Missionaries.

TSTs[29] — The acronym means "**Translucent Space/Time Travelers**". These are the premiere Pilots or Directors of any Planetary craft. They've achieved the evolutionary ability to become translucent or semi-invisible. When these "special greys" are paired with their crafts, ORB, Plate, or V they become one with their craft, without the need for neuro-connectivity. Also called Missionary/Travelers.

When desired, TSTs transit through space/time instantly, no

matter the distance. Their lack of matter eliminates concern for enroute planets, asteroids, space storms or anything else that would otherwise need to be avoided from collisions. They merely **Intimate** a destination from their ORB, Plate, or V craft and they've arrived, instantly. However, typically when accompanying Zoom Mission Convoys, TSTs relinquish their powers of travel and control to the Commanders of Zoom Mission Convoy Fleets.

Visual Beam Portals[30] — External looking lights or port holes on most Plates, and all ORB & V crafts. These beams can be adjusted for many frequencies and intensities. They can appear as beams of any color of light or remain invisible to targets being observed. TST Directors have the ability to capture targets within certain beam intensities and actually beam or lift them aboard a Plate, ORB, or V craft for transport, observations and/or examinations.

Visual Panels[31] — These are more function than objects. When a Plate, ORB, or V craft is switched to Opaque Mode[20], the walls of the craft are completely transparent. As if one is literally standing inside of a glass ball. Glimmering hints of existing objects, like the Command chair, and the Forward-Looking Monitor, are merely clear objects with funny outlines to look through to the outside world.

Zest[32] — The method of modifying or erasing any thought. The natural mind of greys communicates faster than filters can catch. Zesting can recapture thoughts, before they are thought/communicated or transmitted as negative thoughts. (For example, a thought of - "I hate that Picture on the wall", If zested, would become "I must remember to change that picture on the wall, to one that pleases me more.") Additionally, zesting is a way to have an internal thought without it being intimated as telepathic communication.

Zoom Speed[33]— The description given to **Authorized Unlimited Flight Speeds** through Space/Time from point of origin to Final Destination for Plate craft. Typically allowed only in Convoy Fleets between planets, Flash speeds have been more than sufficient for expedited planetary movements for Plates.

Zoom Mission Control[34] — The coordinated group of administrative officials responsible for planning, managing, and contacting or recovering planetary beings that are sought by ABOVE. Plate crafts, under the direction of their convoy Commander, are responsible for Zoom Mission Convoy observations, for either live or subsequent broadcasting of pertinent educational or historical events.